PROBABILITY

CHAIN

PARTS 1-4

(THE COMPLETE FIRST BOOK)

by Regan Keeter

Published by AWG – Roswell, GA

www.regankeeter.com

This book is a work of fiction. Names, characters, places, and
incidents are either the product of the author's imagination or are
use fictitiously. Any resemblance to actual persons living or
dead, events, or locales is entirely coincidental.

FIRST EDITION

Printed in the United States of America

ISBN: 978-0615896489

To my beloved wife, Ana Keeter,
without whom this story would not
have been possible.

As far as the laws of mathematics refer to reality,
they are not certain,
and as far as they are certain,
they do not refer to reality.
— Albert Einstein

CHAPTER 1

When the shape of a young woman began to materialize in the middle of the intersection at Peachtree and Piedmont, six lanes of traffic going more than forty miles-per-hour came to a screeching halt. Car slammed into car as space itself seemed to ripple, to stretch. Although translucent and fuzzy at first, she gained form quickly. And as she did, it became clear to all who could see her that she was badly injured, possibly near death. Hunched over and naked, she held her hands to her bloody neck while cars swerved, horns blared, and steel grinded against steel.

When later questioned by the police, only one of the drivers dared admit that the woman had appeared out of nowhere. The rest claimed they just hadn't seen her.

The answers, though disappointing, were no surprise to the officers. With streetlamps, headlights, lighted billboards, and neon signs making the darkness of night darker and the brightness of light brighter, drivers were often unaware of how little they actually saw once the sun went down.

But, while the question of her origin was important, it was not the question on anybody's mind in the moments that followed her appearance. Instead, the only question

witnesses asked themselves as they stepped from their cars, slack-jawed, was whether this mysterious woman was going to live.

A mother dressed in khaki pants and a blue blouse grabbed a blanket from her trunk and ran toward the stranger, shouting, "Call an ambulance! Somebody call an ambulance, goddammit!"

She kneeled beside the young woman, wrapping the blanket around her and placing her hands on top of the stranger's throat to try to slow the bleeding.

As she did, the young woman looked up at her with desperate blue eyes. Her lips moved to form the name "Brian," but no sound came out.

CHAPTER 2

Several miles away, a heavy, deep thump from downstairs immediately woke Brian Dore. At first he tried to dismiss the sound as meaningless. John Flanders, both clumsy and old, was always dropping one thing or another.

But the sound, hazy and muted, like the dream-soaked, half-memory it was, left him uneasy. For the eleven years Brian had lived with John, he had worried that one day John's clumsiness would send the fragile seventy-five-year-old tumbling down the stairs, not to recover. And when another thump followed, he decided he should investigate.

A small reading lamp sat on the bedside table next to him. He turned it on.

He climbed out of bed and crept into the hall, dressed in his boxers and tee shirt.

He told himself that there was nothing to worry about. John had probably just slipped on the tile floor in the kitchen. Probably making a midnight sandwich when his thin legs came out from under him.

Yet that didn't feel right. Brian couldn't convince

himself to call out for John, ask if he was okay. The uneasiness he'd felt upon waking had grown into a sinking, gnawing feeling twisting in his gut, warning him that the thump had been more than just a fall.

Trying to keep at bay the horrific thoughts that lurked just outside his consciousness, Brian eased quietly along the upstairs hallway. He couldn't bear the thought of something bad happening to the old man. Ever since Brian had moved in, John had treated him like a son, taken care of him, nursed him through the death of his parents.

Underneath the carpet, the floorboards squeaked only once. Brian froze, waited, then kept moving.

Next, he heard a clatter. *Could have been dishes.*

Then a crash. *That wasn't dishes.*

He picked up his pace.

Halfway down the stairs, he remembered the .38 Chief's Special underneath his bed. He cursed himself for not grabbing the gun when he had had the opportunity. But the truth was he rarely thought about it, had never used it. He didn't even know if it worked. He only had it because it had been his father's and was one of the few things left after the fire that had claimed his parents' lives.

Now, closer to the living room than his bedroom, he dared not go back for it. If there were an intruder, moments were precious.

He started back down the stairs. Dark shadows obscured the den below. Only the faint trickle of light that bled through the window in the front door allowed him to see anything at all. He grabbed the handrail for support as if he might faint from fear.

Then he heard a rustling from the kitchen and more clanging: a waterfall of silverware crashing into silverware.

Once on ground level, he could tell that the den was thus far untouched by the intruder. Nothing was in disarray. Everything seemed to be accounted for, including the small TV John frequently watched.

Suddenly a flicker of light from the kitchen caught his attention. A flashlight.

His mind went into overdrive. He knew that whatever he was going to do, he was going to have to do it fast. Any hesitation could be dangerous, possibly deadly.

He swept into the den and grabbed the phone off a small table in the corner. Certain the line would be cut, he placed the receiver to his ear to check for a dial tone. He sighed with relief, punched 9-1-1, and dropped the phone onto the couch.

The operator would be able to trace the call. If nobody spoke, they would assume the worst.

Moving faster now, Brian grabbed Flanders' cane from the hall closet. The cane was made of solid oak and featured a brass handle.

Batter up, he told himself as he swung it over his shoulder, handle in the air. He crept down the hallway toward the kitchen. As he did so, he noticed the rustling sound move to the dining room and the light ahead fade.

Without the glow from the flashlight bouncing off the walls ahead, even the pictures on the faux wood paneling beside him were mere black on black shadows.

He inched forward through the darkness. As he closed the distance between himself and the intruder, his mouth went dry. His palms grew damp. Once he reached the kitchen, only a single doorway would stand between them.

Something on the floor . . .

At first, the thought barely registered. All he could focus on was the danger he was about to encounter.

Something big . . .

He took another cautious step forward, eyes still on the kitchen ahead. Then, the shadowy obstruction found its form and, for a brief moment, Brian stopped thinking about the intruder. For a brief moment, he stopped thinking about anything. He stopped breathing.

With fear gripping his throat, he barely acknowledged the clatter when the cane slipped from his hands and hit the ground. He pawed desperately for the light switch, flipped it.

As sixty blinding watts flooded the hallway, his fears were confirmed.

John Flanders was dead. In his bathrobe. His head was supported by one wall. His legs, bent up at the knee, were jammed into the other. Blood matted his hair, dripped down his face, pooled on the ground beside him.

Nearby lay a bloody wrought-iron candlestick. Brian recognized it as the same candlestick which, until tonight, had occupied a spot in the living room with other knick-knacks.

His hands shook. He stared at the body for a long time, unable to think. Everything around him faded away. In that moment, there was no past, no future, no kitchen before him, no living room behind him . . . just Flanders' body.

Then a sharp pain shot into his brain from the base of his skull and the world came back into focus. He reeled, caught himself before losing his balance, and turned around.

Holding the cane, the intruder took another swing at Brian's head. This time he ducked. Instead of hitting its target, the brass handle tore a hole in the faux wood paneling.

The intruder was wearing khaki pants and a plaid shirt. He'd been smart enough to wear gloves, but hadn't thought to bring a mask. Not even a stocking to obscure his oversized nose and round cheeks. Nothing to hide his quivering brown eyes or greasy black hair.

Subconsciously, Brian understood that it was his lack of preparation that made him so dangerous now.

The burglar jerked the handle out of the wall to take another swing.

Brian jumped back as it took a chunk out of the opposite wall. He lost his balance and fell.

Clearly, the intruder intended on killing him, just as he had John.

Brian could only thank God that the psycho hadn't

come with a gun or he would already be dead.

The gun . . .

His father's gun . . .

If he could get to it . . .

Before he could finish his thought, the intruder swung the cane again. Brian rolled onto his side, as close as he could to the wall, just before the makeshift weapon crashed to the floor.

He knew one more blow from the cane wouldn't kill him, yet it was proving to be as dangerous a weapon as he had expected.

Quickly, he rolled to his feet and backed up several steps, trying to get distance without turning around.

The intruder leapt over the body between them.

Heart pounding, mind blank—no longer thinking or worried about his dead friend, motivated only by his desire to survive—Brian turned to run. But not fast enough. The cane smacked him across the chin. Tearing flesh. Rattling his jaw. Sending him into a spin.

Again, he couldn't keep his feet under him. He fell onto his chest. The impact forced the breath out of his lungs.

A moment later, the cane struck his shoulder, inches from his head. Pain shot up his neck, down his arm. He was lucky the blow hadn't found his skull or he would certainly be unconscious.

But he knew where the next blow would land. He had one last chance for escape. While the intruder raised the cane high, gaining power for the next swing, Brian rolled onto his back and kicked one leg into the air. He caught the intruder in his chest, knocking him away. Then he scrambled to his feet and ran as fast as he could. Past the front door, up the stairs, into his room.

He grabbed a small wooden chair from the corner and wedged it under the door handle. Flanders had only furnished this room with a chair for aesthetic reasons. Except for the rare occasion Brian had used it as a clothes hanger, it had served no other purpose. Until now.

Now it was the only thing standing between him and a violent death.

With the few moments of safety the chair allowed, Brian turned on the overhead light, ran to the bed, collapsed to the floor, and pushed himself against the wall. His head and shoulder throbbed from the previous blows.

The 911 operator had certainly assumed the worst . . .

But what if she hadn't?

The door handle turned. The chair buckled slightly, but held its ground. Then there was a loud thud and the door vibrated violently.

Brian wasn't sure if the intruder had used the cane or his body weight to try to break through. But he knew the door was cheap, hollow. It wouldn't hold up long.

He reached under the bed for the gun. If he had to kill the man, he would. Even if he didn't have to, he might. He could live with the consequences.

John Flanders had been more than just his guardian.

15

He had been Brian's closest friend and confidant. Killing the man who had taken his life would be nothing short of justice.

Another blow to the door.

His hand searched the area where the weapon should be. No gun. Instead, he felt a small piece of paper, probably a receipt that had fallen out of his pocket.

He bent down to look under the bed.

The gun wasn't there!

The receipt, which was sitting exactly where the gun should be, was actually a folded note with his name scribbled on it. The handwriting was very similar to his own, but he knew it wasn't his. Familiar somehow, though not his.

The door vibrated again from another hit.

He grabbed the note, unfolded it, and read the only line that it contained: *The police will get here in time.*

Under different circumstances, this mysterious note might have led him to thoughts about the role fate plays in our lives, about the relationship between destiny and coincidence. But with another thud on the door, wood splintered, revealing one shiny corner of the cane's handle, and his mind went into overdrive as he tried to figure out how he was going to escape.

CHAPTER 3

The police will get here in time.

Brian barely had time to ponder the implications of the note before another blow left a fist-sized opening in the hollow door.

He checked the phone by his bed to see if the 911 operator might still be there, but heard only the beep-beep-beep of a line that had been out of use too long.

Another crack of the cane. More wood splintered from the hollow door. Two more blows and the intruder got his arm through.

Brian scampered over to the windows, still clutching the note. Quickly, he freed the latch and tugged at the handles. Paint had sealed the frame. On the other side of the room, the intruder was pulling at the back of the chair in an attempt to dislodge it. Adrenaline coursed down Brian's arms as he tugged at the window again.

It raised an inch.

The legs of the chair thumped and rattled and then the chair slid to the floor. But before the burglar could open the door and kick it out of his way, Brian managed to get the window all the way open.

He crawled out onto a narrow overhang, glancing back only once.

For a brief second, the intruder had stopped, as if deciding whether to follow Brian into the night. His jaw was clenched.

This was supposed to be a routine burglary, Brian figured.

Just before the intruder decided to give chase, Brian wondered if he should have gone out the front door instead of upstairs. But with the pursuit again on, there was no time to speculate, no use in second-guessing himself. He scrambled down the overhang and readied himself for the twelve-foot jump onto the lawn.

Despite the cold air, tiny beads of sweat formed on his forehead. He looked back at the intruder, who was still inside the house. He tightened his hands into fists. *You can do it. Come on. You can do it*, he told himself. He'd never had any survival training and knew how to manage his landing only from what he'd seen on TV. One mistake and he might break his leg or his wrist. Or worse.

What other options did he have, though? There was no one out walking this time of night. No passing cars he could call to for help.

So he jumped.

Went limp.

His feet hit the ground first. None of his joints were locked. He folded in on himself. Rolled once.

Every bone and muscle hurt, but he didn't think anything was broken.

He got to his feet as quickly as he could and backed up until he could see his window. The intruder was only halfway out.

Finally, he heard sirens.

In his boxers and tee shirt, Brian ran to the street while the intruder retreated into the house. Waving his arms, realizing for the first time he had dropped the note somewhere, Brian flagged down the two black-and-whites. "A burglar," he said once the four officers were out of their cars, "killed John Flanders." This was the first time he had spoken since he'd seen the body. His voice trembled with every word.

"He's still inside?"

Brian nodded.

All four officers pulled their guns. They charged into the house shouting, "Police!"

~

The cops searched the house, repeatedly announcing their presence and encouraging the burglar to surrender. They made mental notes of the damaged door upstairs, the body in the hall, the open rear door, and the broken window inside it.

Outside, Brian waited. He slowly became aware of the chilly night air as goosebumps appeared on his arms and legs. Neighbors turned on lights, stepped out onto porches. Flanders' quiet street was alive with an excitement it had never known before.

Don't think about the body, Brian told himself, trying to shut out the memory of Flanders' bludgeoned skull.

Don't think about the body.

The blood matted in his hair.

Don't think about . . .

"Are you all right, kid?" asked a cop from behind.

A few moments earlier, the officer had come out of the front door and used the radio in his car to broadcast the homicide. Brian hadn't noticed. Startled, he whipped around. He took a deep breath and said, "Yeah, I'm fine. I guess."

"You look a little beat up."

The cop was talking about the wound on his face, Brian realized. Instinctively, he touched his chin. Blood came off on his first two fingers, but not enough to worry him. "It's just a cut."

"We can take you to a hospital."

"I'll be fine."

"Your choice. Anyway, listen, we're going to have to tape off the house. We'll have a forensics team down here soon, and I'm sure a homicide detective will want to talk to you."

Brian glanced around, dazed, swimming in the memory of Flanders' dead body again. "Where are the others?"

"Excuse me?"

"The other cops. There were four, now there's just you." He knew he sounded foolish for asking, but the strange note he had found left him questioning almost everything. He needed confirmation that there had, in fact, been four cops to answer the call. Because if there had only been two, one for each car, then maybe the murder wasn't real and maybe that strange note didn't exist and—

"They're around back. They're still searching for the suspect. Listen, I'm going to go get some clothes for you so you can get dressed, okay? After that . . . well, I'm going to need you to stick around for a while."

Brian nodded. "Sure. Yeah." Then he glanced back at all the neighbors watching the action. "I probably should put on some clothes."

"Where's your room?"

"Top of the stairs. First bedroom you come to."

The cop nodded. "I can pack a small bag for you if you want. You won't be able to get back into the house for a few days."

"Thanks."

"You got any neighbors who would let you stay with them, kid?"

He did, but he wasn't in the mood to discuss the tragedy with his neighbors. Anybody who took him in would keep him up all night with questions. "I'd rather stay in a hotel."

The cop grunted something unintelligible that might or

might not have been sympathetic. Then he hoisted up his belt in an unconscious display of authority and disappeared into the house.

When he returned, the cop was carrying a duffle bag. He directed Brian to his vehicle and opened up the back door. "Climb on in, kid. You'll be more comfortable there than you would be standing around out here. Somebody will be by in a little bit to talk to you."

Brian did as he was told.

The cop handed Brian the duffle bag and walked away.

Mind blank, door open, clutching the duffle bag as if Satan might try to take it from him just as he had taken Flanders, Brian sat. Waited. Behind him, flashing blue and red lights bounced off the two-story Victorian home, a pair of uniforms ran yellow police tape around the property, an ambulance came and left, a forensics team went to work . . .

~

Brian wasn't sure how long he had been sitting in the back of that car before Detective Eric Donaven asked if he could have a word. All he knew for certain was that enough time had passed for most of his neighbors to lose interest and go back inside.

"Sure," Brian said, as emotionless as a machine. The numbness inside still had a chokehold on his pain. Dressed in a tee shirt and jeans, he got out of the car, reluctantly leaving his duffle behind, and shoved his hands into his pockets.

Detective Donaven was a tall man in his late thirties. He was thin, with shallow cheeks and blond hair. Dark, bloodshot eyes betrayed his otherwise spotless appearance — he hadn't sleep well in some time. However, his suit was pressed, his shirt freshly dry cleaned, and his tie was knotted in a double Windsor and pulled to the collar.

In contrast, his partner, Mark Divowlsky, was heavyset, with a round face and a double chin. His movements were slower than Donaven's, and stains on his shirt suggested that he didn't care for his clothing with the same fastidiousness.

"Tell us what happened," Donaven said.

"Well, I was upstairs sleeping when a . . . a thud . . . downstairs woke me up. When I went down to investigate . . . I saw this flashlight moving in the kitchen. That's when I knew . . . for sure . . . something was wrong."

Divowlsky lit a cigarette. "What'd you do then?"

"Well, I had to do something, because I was afraid that something might happen to John if I didn't."

"John?" Donaven asked. "He's . . ."

Brian nodded.

"John what?"

"Flanders."

Donaven scribbled something on a notepad. "He own the house?"

23

"Yes."

"You two related?"

"Uh, no."

"How long have you lived here?"

"Since I was thirteen."

"Thirteen, huh? Where are your parents?"

"John is my guardian. My parents are dead."

"How'd that happen?"

"There was a fire," Brian said, trying not to visualize the ugly aftermath: the charred walls, the torched furniture . . . trying not to remember the nauseating smell of melted plastic that had soaked into the pores of the house.

For months after the accident, Brian had blamed himself for not being home when it happened, but the psychiatrist John had taken him to twice a week had explained there was nothing he could have done to help his parents. The fire appeared to have started in the kitchen. Probably someone had been cooking and had left the stove unattended. From there, the blaze spread up the wallpaper and quickly consumed the house. The autopsy report showed they'd both succumbed to smoke inhalation while trying to make their way down from the second floor. Inevitably, the flames reached them before the firemen could.

Had he been home, he'd likely be dead, too.

"I'm sorry for your loss," Donaven said, solemnly.

"So what did you do when you got downstairs?" Divowlsky pushed.

"I called nine-one-one and . . . and got his cane out of the closet."

"Thinking of taking a stroll?" Divowlsky chuckled at his own joke. His partner shot him a disapproving glance.

To Brian, Donaven said, "Don't pay any attention to him. Go on."

"Anyway, I started down the hall. From the sounds, I could tell the burglar had moved into the dining room. But it made more sense to me to go around, to come up behind him. So I did."

"Armed with a cane," Divowlsky said.

"It was the best weapon I could find."

"Maybe I'm dumb as cow's milk, but I don't get it. If you'd called nine-one-one, why not just duck out of the way and wait for the police to get here? Why go hunting some burglar, who may or may not be armed, with a walking stick?"

Angered by Divowlsky's rude comment, Brian looked up from the sidewalk to meet the detective's eyes. "Because I wasn't sure they'd get here in time."

His gaze drifted away. After several quiet seconds, he continued. "The hallway was dark. I couldn't see the body until I was almost on top of it."

Donaven made another note.

"That's when the burglar attacked. He almost killed me right there in the hallway, but I ran. Upstairs into my room."

"Not outside?"

"Not yet."

"Why not?"

The gun.

"I don't know. . . . Anyway, I shoved a chair under the doorknob. But he just kept pounding at the door until he could get his arm though and push the chair away. So that's when I ran out the window onto the overhang and jumped onto the yard. Then your guys showed up. I think he would have followed me out to the street if the sirens hadn't scared him off."

The detectives glanced at each other. Divowlsky dropped the butt of his cigarette on the sidewalk, crushed it under his toe, and lit another. "You're a lucky boy."

Brian said nothing.

"So you've been here since you were thirteen," Donaven confirmed.

"Uh-huh."

"How old are you?"

"Eighteen."

"Been to college?"

"Not yet."

"Have a job?"

"An internship."

"Where's that?"

"Omega."

"Good company." Another note.

Had Brian been in a better mood, he would have agreed.

Omega Medical was one of the leading drug manufacturers on the East Coast. However to refer to Omega as just a drug manufacturer, as most people did, misrepresented the scope of the company's work. While it was true that Omega was best known for the development of specialized nerve medications, its staff had, since its inception seventeen years ago, also been involved in cancer research and partnered on explorations into alternative medicines.

Brian had been proud when he was offered an internship in the public relations department. So had John. The opportunity to intern at Omega was rare, especially for someone who hadn't graduated college.

"So you were upstairs when you heard a thud," Divowlsky added, ready to get back to the matter at hand.

"That's what I said."

"And it woke you up. . . ."

~

The questions rolled in circles and doubled back on themselves until Brian began to cry. "Can we finish this later?" he asked, his voice cracking. He wiped away his tears and added, "I've already told you everything I know about this. Please, if you want to keep asking me the same questions over and over, can we finish it later? It's been a rough night. I mean, I'm not a suspect, am I?"

Before Divowlsky could tell Brian that this was their

investigation and that they would ask as many questions as they felt like asking, Donaven closed his notepad and said, "I understand." He took a handkerchief from his coat pocket and handed it to Brian.

"Thanks."

"Wait a second," Divowlsky said. "We're not done here."

"For now we are."

"*I'm* not done here."

"Give it a rest, Mark. He's right. He's not a suspect. He's been more than cooperative and he's had a really rough night."

"This is ridiculous. Who's running the investigation here?"

"Mark, why don't you go see what sort of progress forensics has made?"

Divowlsky took a long drag off his cigarette and stormed off.

"Don't pay too much attention to him," Donaven told Brian once his partner was out of earshot. "He's a good investigator, but he's not very compassionate."

"Why's he such a jerk?"

"Just the way he was made," Donaven said. "Come on." Then he started walking toward an unmarked brown sedan.

"Where are we going?"

"You wanted to stay in a hotel tonight, right?"

"I've got a car."

"You're in no condition to drive." He opened up the passenger door. "Come on."

Brian took one last look at the house caged behind yellow police tape. Blue and red lights reflected off its siding. Moving in and out of the front door, officers busied themselves with a variety of tasks.

At that moment, though he couldn't say why, Brian suddenly knew that things were going to get worse.

"Whenever you're ready," Donaven said.

With zero desire to linger, Brian was ready. He got his duffle bag out of the back of the police car and joined the detective in the sedan.

They pulled out onto the road. Donaven asked, "What hotel do you want to go to?"

"There's an Embassy Suites on Clifton."

"Yeah, I know it."

As they traversed the city, neither of them said a word. The only sound in the car came from the relentless static and fuzzy voices on the police radio. Outside his window, Brian watched the endless procession of street lamps until his tears dried up. When the silence became too much for him, he said, without turning his head, "John was a good man."

Donaven, unsure if Brian was talking to himself or to him, replied anyway. "I'm sure he was."

"He used to be a doctor."

"A noble profession."

"Everyone liked him. All the neighbors . . . everyone."

They turned right onto Clifton.

"Sounds like a great man."

Then the car fell silent again. The silence seemed to swell with pain, making the air thick, hard to breathe.

Donaven rolled down his window to let in a fresh breeze. The pressure in the car subsided some.

"Try to get some sleep," the detective said after pulling up in front of the hotel and giving his passenger a business card.

Brian got out of the car, smiled weakly back, and said he would. He dropped the handkerchief on the passenger seat and, with his duffle bag slung over one shoulder, went into the lobby.

CHAPTER 4

It was going on two-thirty A.M. The tragedy had already sucked three hours out of Brian, but now—instead of sleeping—he was sitting in his hotel room, mindlessly watching TV. Some sort of low-budget thriller about the drug trade. A guy on the screen, whose name he hadn't caught, had just filled a cut-off latex finger with cocaine and swallowed it to get the drugs through customs.

During the commercial break, his eyes drifted to the bottle of pills on the dresser.

The concierge had given him a sealed, brown envelope when he checked in and he'd found the bottle of pills inside.

"Here. Somebody left this for you."

As he studied the bottle, wondering who had left it, his mind retreated from reality to an almost dream-like state, plunging him back through fractured memories until it latched onto a conversation at the office earlier that day. Talk of a new drug. Very hush-hush. Nobody knew exactly what it was, what it did, but there were

31

theories. . . .

"I don't know what they call it," said Shawn Ryder, an employee in the PR department. Then, hovering around Brian's desk, he glanced over his shoulder to make sure nobody was listening. "But I've heard it does wild things."

"Like what?"

"Jerry, you know, one of the janitors, thinks it might be like LSD, only way more intense."

"What would Omega be doing making something like LSD?"

Shawn picked up the stapler off Brian's desk and played with it nervously. Most of the staff had already heard this story, but Brian knew that Shawn liked pretending they hadn't. "How should I know? Omega's into all kinds of stuff."

"Nothing against Jerry, but I don't think he's qualified to make these sorts of assumptions. Neither are we."

Shawn's face scrunched up tight with frustration. He put Brian's stapler down and leaned forward on the desk. Keeping his voice at a whisper, he said, "Well, whatever it is, it sounds damn interesting, I'll tell you that for sure."

Then Kerri White, the redheaded manager of the PR department, stopped by Brian's desk to deliver a press release. "It sounds like science fiction to me, boys. Omega wouldn't waste its time with something like that." She spoke with a smile that showed all her teeth and was wearing a skirt that showed most of her legs. Everyone knew she had gotten the job for her looks, but she'd since *proven to be as smart as she was beautiful.*

Shawn jerked his head around. He hadn't heard anyone coming and was surprised to see her there. "Well, of course you'd say that."

"Jerry's a halfwit who overheard some midnight conversation and took it out of context."

Shawn scoffed in her direction, but said nothing. He and Kerri had never gotten along. She was too levelheaded for him and never took part in his conspiracy theories.

"By the way, the drug's called Diaxium," she said, just before leaving. "That is, if you believe Jerry."

Although the container on the dresser probably didn't contain Diaxium, there was no name printed on it. It could have been anything.

There was also a note inside the envelope. Written on hotel stationary, the note said simply: *Take one as soon as you can. Trust me. A friend.*

The same handwriting from the note under his bed. Even though the first one had accurately told him the police would arrive in time, he had not yet decided whether to trust this mysterious prophet.

He knew I would go for the gun. He knew I would come to this hotel. What does he want? How could he know?

But it was not just the unexplainable notes and the vanishing gun that alarmed Brian. It was also, to a lesser degree, his missing cash. While he had expected to pay for

33

the room with a credit card, he hadn't expected to be missing the twenty dollars he'd gotten from an ATM earlier that day.

He glanced from the TV to the pills to the TV to the pills.

I don't know what they are.

He thought about Flanders' bloody skull and his parents dead on the stairs . . .

I don't even know where they're from.

. . . the flames burning up the wallpaper, consuming the ceiling . . .

They could be dangerous.

. . . the closed caskets at the funeral . . .

In the mood I'm in now, I . . .

. . . the charred remains of the house . . .

. . . shouldn't . . .

. . . and he wished he'd never stopped taking the anti-depressants the psychiatrist had prescribed for him after his parents died. When Brian's life had transitioned out of the darkness of loss, when he had started thinking not about a future of what might have been, but of what might be, the doctor had weaned him off the medication.

Now he needed them more than he ever had. And if he couldn't get them, he needed something, anything, to take away his pain. Cyclobenzaprine, dopamine, nortriptyline, doxepin, anything! Suddenly he wanted to trust this strange prophet.

. . . mustn't . . .

Could it really be that much worse than reality?

No, it couldn't.

He lunged for the container of pills and shook one out into his trembling hand. Discovering they were chalky to the touch, he chased it down with a glass of water from the bathroom sink.

He needed to escape, just for a little while. No matter where he went, no matter what sort of dreams he'd have, he needed to get away from his thoughts.

He put the "Do Not Disturb" sign on the exterior door handle to make sure nobody would walk in on him. Then he sat on the edge of his bed, waiting for the drug to kick in.

Five minutes passed.

He remembered the bloody candlestick.

Sweat broke out on his brow. He began to worry he had made a mistake by taking the pill.

Before he had a chance to dwell on it, though, his stomach clenched. He lurched forward, hands wrapped around his torso. Then he fell to the floor and started to spasm. His throat seized up. Suddenly, he couldn't breathe. The convulsions grew worse. His heart raced. His eyes rolled back. The room disappeared into blackness.

When the seizures stopped, unconsciousness followed.

CHAPTER 5

Brian was overcome with the need to vomit when he awoke. The uncontrollable urge welled up from his gut. He pushed himself onto his hands and knees. Stomach acid and chunks of food burned his throat as he expelled the filth onto a dirty cement floor.

Accompanying some sort of harsh, industrial music, he could see flashing strobes against his closed eyelids, and then, eyes open, the cracked cement underneath him.

Immediately, he realized he was no longer in his hotel room. Equally disturbing, he also realized he was naked.

As his gaze followed the cracks in the floor outward, he saw he was surrounded by an assortment of shoes he couldn't identify. Many were made of thick, black leather, reminiscent of Army boots.

He wiped his chin, lifted his head.

The men and women around him were dirty. Most wore clothes made of leather or cotton that had been cut close to the body and showed signs of age. Sleeves were unraveling. Pants were torn.

Nearby, water dripped through a hole in a pipe,

forming a puddle.

Where was he? What had happened to him?

The drug.

None of this was real. It couldn't be. He was dreaming.

The breeze shifted. He smelled rotting meat. His stomach turned, but he didn't get sick.

Staring and pointing, the imaginary people chatted among themselves. But with the music overhead deafeningly loud, he could not hear what they were saying.

Then a young woman stepped forward. She kneeled beside him. She was dressed in tight leather pants that had a rip down one thigh, a leather jacket, and a gray shirt made of burlap . . . or something like it. She tucked her long black hair over her shoulder. *"Su bastu di?"* she shouted at him in a language he couldn't understand.

She waited while he rotated on his knees to face her. When he didn't answer, she grabbed his right hand and turned it over to look at the back of it.

The music stopped. No house lights came on.

"Lo nisti?" asked someone from the crowd.

"Nal lati lo," she answered.

"What are you saying?" Brian asked.

Before she could respond, if she even understood him, the east wall exploded inward. Cinderblocks crumbled as clouds of dust filled the air. Half-a-dozen motorcycles, mounted with blinding headlights, roared through the opening.

37

People around him screamed and scattered in all directions. They pushed past each other, around each other, and trampled the fallen in an attempt to escape. Shots were fired and somebody howled in pain as a bullet tore through his thigh.

The woman grabbed Brian's arm. *"Hord da li,"* she insisted. *"Hord da li!"*

From her tone, he translated that as "Come with me," and he did.

As she pulled him to his feet, he realized his legs were almost too weak to run. He struggled to keep up. Had she let go of his arm at any point, he would have lost her. He would have fallen behind, dropped to his knees, been trampled like so many others.

His heart pounded with fear. He tried to remind himself none of this was real. After it was all over, he would be back in the hotel room where he started, he told himself. Back with the loneliness and the pain . . .

When gunfire whizzed past nearby, his fear put a halt to these thoughts.

The woman led him behind the bar and pushed aside a liquor cabinet to reveal a hole in the floor. She threw herself feet-first through it like she'd done it a thousand times and shouted at him—to follow, he assumed. He did, albeit much less gracefully.

They landed inside a tunnel. The woman grabbed a thin slab of cement off the ground. With one quick motion, she used the iron handle on the bottom to twist it into the hole like a screw. She pulled a small flashlight from her boot. As she did, he noticed something taped to the back of her hand. Then she grabbed Brian's arm again and continued to run.

The cement hallways were narrow, making him feel claustrophobic. But all too soon she led him up a ladder, through a small grate, onto the street outside.

The city looked like a war zone. Buildings were crumbling. The streets were dirty. Neon signs flashed from behind bared windows. Trash, caught in drafts, blew aimlessly. Many streetlamps didn't work; others just flickered. At night, the city was scary. If it had been real, Brian would have been absolutely terrified.

Panicking, he was unable to absorb any details before another explosion cracked the walls of the club behind them. They ran. Fast.

After several blocks, she pointed to a distant building and said something else in that strange tongue. However, as before, he was able to discern meaning from her tone and gestures. That building was their destination.

Unfortunately, the farther they went, the weaker he felt. His stomach started to turn again. The blood rushed out of his legs. He dropped to all fours only a block from the building. The shaking started. The spasms came soon after.

"Traca cano sta do? Traca stor?"

His eyes rolled back in his head and everything disappeared.

CHAPTER 6

Brian awoke to a loud *BANG! BANG! BANG!* on the door of his hotel room. It was relentless—and magnified by his throbbing headache. He rolled to his knees. Before he could speak, his stomach turned. Acid burned up into his throat as he hung his head over the side of the bed, but nothing else followed.

Like in his dream, he was naked. His clothes lay haphazardly on the floor nearby. The TV was still on, canned laughter pouring out of tiny speakers.

From the other side of the door: "Brian, this is Detective Donaven! Open up!"

Morning already? He staggered to the door through the sun-bleached room. Squinting eyes and voice hoarse, he said, "Let me put some clothes on, all right? Just a second."

The banging stopped.

Brian turned off the TV, grabbed his clothes, and sat down on the end of the bed. After dressing in everything but his socks, he noticed the dirt caked to the bottoms of his feet. Street dirt. It must have gotten there after he

40

jumped out of his bedroom window.

How he wished he had time for a shower.

Donaven: "Come on, hurry up!"

He slipped on his socks and was about to get the door when he saw the bottle of pills. He didn't want to have to explain anything, so he hid them inside the top dresser drawer.

"Where the hell were you yesterday?" Donaven asked, after Brian finally let him in.

"What do you mean?"

"I mean Divowlsky and I came by, just like I told you we would. We knocked on this door until we just about broke it down. Finally, I had to get the front desk clerk to let us in. You weren't here."

"What day is it?"

Donaven put his hands on his hips, pushing back his suit jacket as he did so. Clearly he was not in a good mood. "Tuesday. What day do you think it is?"

The murder had happened on Sunday night. The only way it could be Tuesday is if he had been unconscious for more than thirty hours. "You must have had the wrong room."

"Don't play games with me. I'm not in the mood."

If you'd had the right room, you would have found me on the bed. Naked. . . . When did I take off my clothes?

"Well, I'm here now. Where's your partner?"

"He couldn't make it."

Brian nodded. "So you want to go through the

41

questions again?" His eyes had adjusted to the sunlight, but he was still tired and his head still ached.

"Don't need to. Something's come up."

"What?"

"You know a girl named Raven?"

Brian thought hard, back through his memory. "No."

"Yeah, well, she knows you. She wants to talk to you real bad, too. She's down at Piedmont Hospital in ICU. Came in Sunday night with her throat slit and a busted knee cap."

"Wait a second, you don't think *I* . . ."

"She says you're a friend, that's all. She's not accusing you of anything. But I can't help wondering if there might be a connection between what happened to her and the robbery at your place. Call it a cop's instinct."

"You think I'm that connection?"

"I don't think you're responsible, if that makes you feel any better. However, I'd be real interested to see what happens if I get you two together to talk."

Brian shifted nervously on the bed as that ominous feeling—the sense that something bad was lurking just beyond the horizon—returned. "She really wants to talk to me that badly, huh?"

"You're the only one she's willing to talk to."

"All right," Brian said, realizing he didn't have a choice, "let's go." He followed the detective out of the room, rode down the elevator with him, and walked through the underground parking lot to his car.

Donaven flashed his badge at the parking attendant and the attendant waved him through.

The day was warm. Brian rolled down his window to let in some fresh air.

"You know, she's really a lucky girl," the detective finally said.

"How so?"

"Whoever sliced her up took out her vocal chords. Lucky for her, they missed both major arteries. I'm not a doctor, but I'm pretty sure if either of those had been hit, she'd be dead. I still don't get why some dumb fucker would dump her out in the middle of an intersection, though. Maybe he didn't have the balls to finish the job himself and he thought somebody would just run her over. Boom. That would be that."

Brian sighed, but said nothing. As a cop, Donaven had offered up more information than he should have. He was sharing details that Brian didn't want to know.

"One eyewitness said she just appeared out of thin air, literally," the detective continued. ". . . if you can believe that." He chuckled and shook his head.

They pulled into the parking lot and were soon on the third floor of the hospital. Dr. Stort, a short, hairy man with hairy palms, led them into Raven's room.

She was surrounded by machines that seemed to live and breathe with her, for her. Bandages hid stitches on her neck. Her right leg, from thigh to toe, was in a cast.

She turned her attention away from the television

when they entered and smiled when she saw Brian. "That's the first smile I've seen from her," Donaven said, as she waved them over.

Cautiously, Brian approached.

Raven reached for the pen and pad on the bedside table.

Hi, she wrote.

"I should warn you, she has trouble with her spelling."

"Hi," Brian said.

Ivv meised yoou, she wrote.

"Do you recognize her now?"

Brian stared hard, reluctant to say he didn't. He could see the desperation in her silvery eyes. She wanted him to remember her. And, to be honest, she looked vaguely familiar. To be completely honest, she looked like the woman in his dream. But dreams, he knew, had no place in a police investigation.

"I don't think so."

Tri, she wrote.

"I'm sorry. I wish I did," he told the detective. "Anything I could do to find John's killer, you know I would. Where should I know her from?"

Donaven shrugged, disappointed.

Raven wrote: *lost angls*

"Where?" he asked her.

Lst engles

Brian looked at Donaven. "I'm sorry I can't be more help." He took a step back.

Raven wrote with desperation: *Waite dont goe Dont goe*

"I can't help you. I wish I could. I do," he said sadly. Then to Donaven: "Both of you. You know I do."

Dont goe

Brian backed toward the door. "I don't know who you are." He turned to leave and she threw the writing supplies at him. The doctor, who'd remained all but invisible until now, ducked. The pen smacked against the wall. The notepad fluttered and tumbled to the floor.

Brian moved faster now, almost racing for the door, and Donaven followed him out.

Back in the room, Raven opened her mouth in a silent, frustrated scream.

CHAPTER 7

Shawn Ryder was quick to notice that Brian was missing on Monday and quick to share the news with the rest of the PR staff at Omega.

"Probably just the flu," Kerri White told Shawn in the break room when he mentioned it to her. She brushed her long red hair away from her face and poured a cup of coffee.

"Yeah, I'm sure that's it," Shawn said. His eyes grew wide. "But what if he was abducted? Like by aliens or something?"

"Oh, don't start in with your stories again. He's probably just sick."

Heating a Pop Tart in the microwave, a portly, shy man from accounting listened but didn't speak.

"Or what if something really bad happened?" Shawn continued. "What if—"

"Stop it, okay? You're being ridiculous. I do wish he'd call, though, and tell us so we'd know how much of his slack we're going to have to pick up." She sipped her coffee and walked out of the room.

But by Tuesday, even Kerri, who had been running the PR department for the last three months, was concerned. She called his home, got no answer, and finally resigned herself to the fact that he might not return. Maybe he had quit . . . or walked out, so to speak.

Suddenly, Timothy Maine, CEO of Omega, charged through the glass door that divided the PR department from the rest of the building. He huffed and puffed with exhaustion. Rage twisted his round, pudgy face and his skin was burning red.

With two security guards in tow, he stopped when he could see that Brian was not at his desk, then barked at Shawn: "Where is Mr. Dore?"

Shawn sank low in his chair. "I don't know. I haven't seen him."

Maine made a sharp right, with the guards still behind, and threw open the door to Kerri's office. He repeated his question.

"He hasn't been in today," she said, struggling to keep her composure. Maine was rude and unpredictable. That unpredictability made him intimidating.

"What about yesterday? He wasn't here yesterday, either, was he?"

"No," she said.

He sneered and stormed out of the department, cursing.

~

Not thirty minutes ago, Maine had been sitting in his office, tucked comfortably into his big leather chair, enjoying his morning coffee. It had been looking like it was going to be a good morning. *The Wall Street Journal*, which was spread out across his oak desk, had reported his stocks were up. His dog Stew had managed the night without taking a dump on his floor.

You have to take joy in the little things, he said, because the big things take too much time.

His phone rang.

Security had been reviewing the tapes from the weekend. Standard procedure. There was never anything unusual on them. Because of that, the security staff always took their time getting around to the work.

Never . . . until now.

"You need to get down here right away," Security Officer Bob Jenkins told Maine. "We've had a break-in."

"Where?"

"Sub-level."

Maine nearly choked on his coffee and hung up. *Sub-level?* His heart began to pound. *What the . . . ?*

This wasn't going to be a good morning, after all.

On the way out of his office, he told his secretary to call Steven Lester and have him come down to security. But he didn't slow down to wait for her response or reaction.

Steven Lester was the twitching, stuttering genius

behind Omega, the man who'd made even the company's most unlikely projects a success. He was the only scientist Maine had ever known who shared the CEO's unhealthy interest in, well, certain subjects that neither man discussed outside of Maine's office or The Lab.

Sub-level.

Save Maine and Lester, only the guards at Omega knew it existed. The only camera down there watched a plain white hallway and a door that was always closed. No further security had been necessary. Not only were the secrets of that room guarded from all eyes, you needed a key to send the elevator to the sub-level and an access code to get through the door at the end of the hall.

When Maine reached the security room, which was not much bigger than a glorified closet, Steven was already there waiting for him. Crowded by monitors and a stack of digital recorders, the four of them—Maine, Lester, and the two guards—barely fit.

"What have we got?" he asked.

"One man. Male. Coming out."

"In, t-t-too, right?" Steven asked. He looked frazzled. His short brown hair, normally carefully parted, was a mess. Behind his glasses, his eyes seemed to have retreated deeper into his skull.

"No sir, just out."

Timothy Maine and Steven Lester shared a quick and meaningful look. But just as fast, Maine dismissed the guard's statement as an error. Since there was only one way in or out, they must have overlooked the intruder's arrival—or not reviewed enough of the tape.

"Play it," Maine demanded, and a guard clicked a button on the keyboard. The counter on the upper-left monitor began to tick off seconds.

After a moment, the lab door opened. Both Timothy and Steven knew their intruder from just a glance.

Brian Dore. Dressed only in a long white lab coat. Carrying a pill bottle.

"H-H-Holy . . ."

"This is a problem," Maine said.

"A big one," Steven agreed.

"He remembers the room."

"Apparently."

"But how'd he get in?" Maine asked softly, mostly to himself. Then, in a more demanding voice, he told Steven, "Find out what he took."

To the guards: "Come with me."

~

Having seen the tape, Maine wasn't surprised that Brian hadn't come to work. He sent the guards back to their posts and returned to his office. His first call went out to John Flanders.

By God, *somebody* should have told him about Brian's absence. As a secret employee of Omega, that old man was responsible for reporting any unusual behavior.

No answer.

His second call went out to a guy who called himself "Rock." Rock had been a professional boxer for five years and had the mangled, flat nose to prove it. After a ruptured spleen forced his early retirement, he had moved into private investigation.

However, it was neither his size nor brutality Maine most prized. He was a man without morals. So were the men he hired. For Maine, this was invaluable.

"I've got a job for you," he said into the phone, and slid one hand across the top of his bald head. A ring of gray hair that ran ear to ear was all he had left from his once-impressive blond locks. "I've got an address I need you to check out."

"Sure thing, Mr. Maine. We'll get right on it."

Of course they would. Rock and his associates always gave Maine's problems top priority. Rightly they should, Maine would have said. The CEO paid them three times their normal rate to ensure both their expediency and their discretion.

Tight lips were important when dealing with problems as delicate as his. Problems like his could not be discussed in polite society. He was trying to change the world—for the better, mind you, but . . .

Well, people simply wouldn't understand.

They don't spank kids in school anymore. Even spanking one at home was frowned upon. People were too tolerant these days. Sure, they wanted their fancy homes and their fancy cars, their streets free of crime and their bodies made well when they got sick, but they didn't want to know what dark beasts made those things possible.

After Maine gave Rock the address, he said, "I want the house secured as soon as you arrive. If Mr. Dore's there, hold him until the close of business, then bring him to me. If Flanders is there, find out why he hasn't called."

"I'm on it."

"You bet you are."

~

"I don't know who she is. I don't know why she asked for me," Brian stammered.

He and Donaven were standing in the hall just outside Raven's room when the doctor came out of the door behind them. "I'm sorry, I don't know what's wrong with her," he said. "She hasn't acted like that since she's been here."

"I don't know what she wants from me."

"Calm down," Donaven said. "Take it easy."

Brian ran his hands down his cheeks, tried to nod.

"Why'd you get so freaked out back there?"

"I don't know."

The doctor stepped back to a respectful distance, but not out of earshot. A pack of nurses scurried past, giggling about one thing or another.

"Because she got so mad," Brian added.

Donaven's hands were back on his hips again. "That's all?"

"Well, she did look"—*vaguely like*—"sorta familiar. But I really don't know why."

"All right, take it easy. I'm going to need you to go back in there so I can find out what she has to say—"

"I can't go back in there. You saw how she acted . . ."

"Look, son, you will go back in there. I've got a murder to solve. You need—"

"I can't."

"You'll do it in handcuffs if that's what it takes!" Donaven snapped.

~

Maine hung up the phone and began pacing, his thoughts sifting through his mind too fast to make sense. He stopped at the small bar by his couch, poured a tall bourbon, and downed half of it before Steven came into the room.

Steven looked more alarmed than he had before, though Maine couldn't have said exactly how. Maybe it was because his movements seemed more abrupt. Or maybe it was the slight tremor in his hands. "Jesus," he said. "F-F-F-Flyin' Mary, mother of Jesus."

After another gulp of bourbon, Maine put the glass on his desk. "What?"

"He took a bottle of the Diaxium. There are still two

more, but . . ."

Maine sighed with frustration. "Do you think he knows what it does?"

"Do I n-n-need to remind you? We don't even know what it does."

Steven was right. All they had were theories, largely based on Princeton physicist Hugh Everett III's "Many Worlds" idea.

In 1957, Hugh Everett published his "Many Worlds" idea to better explain the relationship between the microscopic and macroscopic worlds. Until that time, it was generally agreed that the former only had meaning by what we observed in the latter, which is the world we interact with daily.

To do this, he created the universal wave function, which allowed him to determine all possible quantum object configurations.

What Lester found especially interesting about his work was that this wave function, which is still used by physicists today, illustrated that everything which can happen, does happen. Quantum physics explains that, before we interact with or observe the particles that make up the world around us, they are actually in *all possible places* at the same time.

Since, within one dimension, we can't actually observe these particles in more than one place, previous theory arbitrarily claimed that all possibilities collapse to only one possibility when we interact with it. It was a way of dealing with an issue that couldn't otherwise be explained. Everett, however, claimed that it is in the space just before every interaction with the world around us when new dimensions are born. In that small window of time, we assume a relationship with those particles, and every other possible relationship with those particles spawns a new dimension where the alternative relationship exists.

And he provided the mathematics to prove it.

Therefore, Lester wondered, if every possibility throughout history that can happen has happened, why should we be privy to only one timeline when it is actually sandwiched between an uncountable number of others? If we could trigger our molecules to behave differently, effectively tune our brains to align with a different set of probabilities, he theorized, we may be able to shift our entire bodies to a neighboring timeline.

Most likely, any variation of the drug would shift us to the same timeline consistently since it would continue to tune us in to that same probability chain.

The implications of successfully developing such a drug were almost unfathomable. It was exactly the kind of global game changer that got Maine and Lester excited. Diaxium could bring them scientific notoriety, of course, but Maine was also confident that it could net billions from government agencies interested in using it for military applications.

"Jumping from this world to that world and back

would give a whole new meaning to sneaking up on your enemy," he'd told Steven.

So far, though, they'd only tested the drug on rats. Initial results were promising, but inconclusive.

After ingesting the drug, the rats had vanished. Contorted, sick, they had faded into thin air, suggesting a shift from one dimension to another as Lester had hoped.

Unfortunately, not all of them returned. Of those that did, many returned mangled and half-dead.

So what could Brian want with the pills? How could he even know about them?

Jerry.

Or the room?

He remembers.

But what could he want with them? And, more importantly, how did he get in?

These were the questions that had to be answered.

~

Reluctantly, Brian went back into Raven's room. Her hands had relaxed from knotted fists. She was staring blankly at the wall in front of her. As soon as she heard the door, she turned. Her face lit up. She tried to say something, but Brian couldn't read her lips. With urgent desperation, she mimicked writing something.

Donaven looked from the pad and pen on the floor to Brian and back. "Go on," he prodded.

The doctor slipped in behind them.

More cautious than he'd been before, Brian picked up the writing supplies. He carried them over to Raven. She took them greedily and scribbled out on a fresh page: *Dnt go*

"There was something you wanted to tell him," Donaven reminded her. "Something you would tell only him. What was that?"

She looked from the cop to Brian to the paper to Brian, and turned over a fresh sheet on the pad. Then, again, in big letters: *Dont go*

The more Brian tried to figure out why she looked so familiar, the more he realized she resembled the woman from his dream.

"We're not going to leave you just yet," Donaven said.

She turned over another page, and wrote with even bigger letters—

Ddont ggo

Dontt go

Doont goe

CHAPTER 8

"'Don't go.' That's all she kept writing over and over again," Brian told Shawn later that evening. They were sitting in the hotel's restaurant, drinking coffee.

Shawn was one of the few people Brian spent time with other than John. They had bonded over their shared love of tennis and, until recently, had a standing Sunday match. As time passed, he'd come to enjoy Shawn's imaginative stories, even though they often bordered on the absurd. They seemed to color the world in a way that gave every action more meaning than it had on its own. Today, though, Brian needed a sympathetic ear, not conspiracy theories.

"What do you think it meant?" Shawn asked, glancing nervously around. He still had on the blue and white, striped button-down he'd worn to the office, but he had taken off his tie and freed the top two buttons.

"How should I know?"

Shawn glanced to his right again at a nearby diner, sitting by himself, reading a newspaper. "Well, that's not the only strange thing that's happened today. You better be glad you didn't come into the office."

"What happened?"

"Kerri was fired. I was manning her office all afternoon."

"Fired? What for?"

"For not telling Mr. Maine you were absent. Can you believe that? I've seen him go off the deep end before, but today he went nuts. Totally nuts."

"Maybe if I let him know why I've been gone—"

"No way. He had security with him when he came looking for you. That's how he found out you weren't there. He wants your butt bad."

Brian's stomach knotted and he pushed the coffee away. "What for? I haven't done anything to him."

"Jerry got fired too, I heard." Shawn took a sip from his cup. "Bet it had something to do with that conversation he overheard."

"Don't get started on that again."

"I'm just saying—"

"Well, don't."

"Whatever's going on at Omega, Mr. Maine is furious. Heads are rolling, man. I mean really rolling."

"Yeah, I got it."

"So, go ahead. I'm curious. What have you done to make him so mad?"

"Nothing," Brian said defensively. "I don't know why he's mad."

"He showed up with security guards looking for you

and you don't know why he's mad?"

"I'd tell you if I did."

"Yeah, well, maybe you would, maybe you wouldn't."

"Let's assume that I would."

They both stopped talking, and a man to their left, alone and reading a book, cleared his throat. Shawn glanced at him, then back at the stranger reading his paper.

"I think you should stay with me tonight. I've got a fold-out couch. It's not fancy, but you'd be comfortable."

"I appreciate that . . . I think I'd just prefer to be alone. Don't get me wrong, I'm glad you came by."

"I think you're making a mistake." Shawn leaned in and whispered, "I'm worried about you. I think we're being watched."

More conspiracy theories.

More fairytales.

"I'm serious." His eyes darted to the right. "The man with the newspaper over there." To the left. "The man with the book over there." Back at Brian. "And one behind you. He's been working on the same drink since I arrived."

"Shawn."

"I'm just—"

"Listen to me."

"—worried."

"This is a big hotel in a big city. They're probably just here on business. Please . . . please don't start in with more of your stories. Not right now."

"But everything at the office . . . And Mr. Maine is a

powerful man."

"I haven't done anything to him. How would he find me at the hotel, anyway?" Brian signed the slip the waiter had left and billed the drinks to his room. He stood up, his chair squealing loudly against the wooden floor as he slid it back. All three men glanced briefly at him. So did a couple at another table.

"Don't stay here tonight," Shawn pleaded, now standing, as well.

"I'll call you tomorrow."

"What if—"

"I will."

The notes, the pills, the girl, the gun . . . No, don't let his stories inside. Not right now. I have enough of my own problems right now. Nobody's watching me.

"You know," Brian continued, "you should think about chilling out on the stories you tell. You know they're just fun and games, right?"

Shawn smirked as if it were a joke. "Maybe I do, maybe I don't." Then he winked.

They shook hands and Brian walked away. "Thanks for stopping by."

"You better get in touch with me tomorrow," Shawn called after him. He glanced one last time at each of the three men—they were a mean-looking bunch.

Shrugging off his suspicion, he headed through the lobby to the front exit.

~

But Brian had let the stories inside.

At the rear of the lobby, he pressed the elevator button and glanced back at the restaurant. The men were still there. A bald man reading his newspaper. A crew cut behind a book. Shaggy blond hair at the bar.

They're not watching me.

The elevator doors opened and he rode back up to his floor.

He'd spent all afternoon in his room. Trying to sleep. Twirling the bottle of pills in his hand. Wondering who had left it.

Now, he would try to sleep again. He would try not to think about Flanders, Maine, Shawn, Raven, the note . . .

Everything would make more sense after a good night's sleep.

He stripped to his boxers, turned off the light, and crawled under the covers.

They weren't watching me.

Then his door opened.

CHAPTER 9

The three men had wandered into the restaurant casually, one after the other, several minutes apart. The man with the bald head and flattened nose had been first. Then, his associate with shaggy blond hair. Finally, the crew cut.

Finding Brian had not been without its challenges, but it hadn't been the most difficult job Rock and his partners had done, either.

The journey had begun, of course, at Flanders's house. Though there was no activity there at the time, police tape still marked off the property.

Dressed in a suit, Rock ducked under the tape, put on a pair of black leather gloves, and went in through the unlocked door. Nobody was on the street to observe him. Inside, despite the gloves, he touched nothing.

Enough light filtered in through the windows to make all the rooms visible. Floorboards squeaked under his feet.

He quietly examined each room. The phone was still off the hook in the den. Blood stained the wall and the floor in the hallway.

The kitchen was in shambles. Drawers open. Silverware on the floor. Broken dishes. The overhead lamp was shattered.

Upstairs he found the hole torn into Brian's door; his bedroom window was still open.

When he got back to the car, he called his office.

"Bernhard and Associates," a man answered.

Rock, born Allen Bernhard, looked out his windshield and saw a little girl pull out of a garage on her bike and peddle away. Into the phone, he said, "Frankie."

"You know it, pal. What's up?"

"I need you to get in touch with your guys on the force. Find out what happened at the Flanders address."

"Sure thing. Call you back in ten?"

"Make it five, if you can." Then Rock hung up, turned the key in the ignition until it clicked once, and listened to the radio while he waited for his phone to ring. The little girl on the bike rode back down the street, grinning and laughing. She passed him, turned around, and rode back up again.

"Screw it."

He headed back toward the office. There was no good reason to sit in his car beside a crime scene waiting for a phone call.

~

Just after turning onto Tenth Street, Rock got the call

from Frankie Munch that he'd been waiting for. Frankie was an ex-cop, homicide, so getting information usually didn't take long.

He reported the murder to Rock, but said he couldn't find out Brian's whereabouts. Asking for those specifics might raise suspicion from his contacts. Besides, with Rock's second and final associate a computer whiz, a notable hacker at twelve and one of the best in the world at thirty, they didn't need the cops to get Brian's location.

Rock told Frankie to get Crow Gartner, the computer whiz, working on it.

"He's on his way back now," Frankie said.

"From where?"

"He was watching Mrs. Martinez's husband, remember? The suspected affair?"

That's right. The affair. Researching suspected infidelity was beneath them, but it made up much of their work.

"Don't worry," Frankie continued, "I've already called Hubbard Investigators and got a sub out there for him." Hubbard regularly covered their excess business. "It's just a watch-and-shoot job right now, so any ape they send out there can do it."

"How long will it take him to get back?"

"He should be walking through the door any second."

Rock pulled to a red light. "Fine. Get him working on the brat's location as soon as he walks in the door."

"Will do."

~

Rock's firm was located on the third floor of an old brick building downtown. Other occupants of the building included insurance agencies and a new law firm.

In the twelve hundred square feet Rock had claimed as his, the linoleum tile had started to peel at the corners. The walls needed a new coat of paint. Each of his associates had his own office, but they spent most of their time huddled together in Rock's. No receptionist had sat up front for more than a year; a bell tied to the door announced visitors as effectively as she had.

"I've got it!" Crow shouted. Frankie, still wearing the buzz cut he'd first donned during his years on the force, was in his office seconds later. So was Rock.

Crow had accessed Brian's credit cards with relative ease. "He's at The Embassy Suites. Even got the address for you."

Rock picked up the receiver of Crow's desk phone and called Maine. Now that he had more than just the murder to report, he was prepared for the conversation.

"What have you got for me?" Maine asked.

"Good and bad."

"So? What is it?"

"First, I guess you should know John Flanders is dead."

Maine, who didn't seem even mildly upset by

Flanders's death, just asked if they'd located Brian.

"Yes, we have. He's staying at a hotel near John's house."

"Good. The rest of your men are there with you?"

"Yes, sir."

"Put me on speakerphone."

Rock did.

"I want you guys to get down to the hotel, but don't do anything stupid," Maine said. "Find him. Watch him. When it's quiet, bring him to me. And, by God, find the pills he took, too."

And that is exactly what they did.

As Maine had expected, there were too many people in the parking garage, the hallways, and the lobby to do anything but wait. Theirs were not faces they wanted remembered.

One at a time, they followed Brian into the restaurant. If he tried to bolt, they would nab him then, regardless of how it might look. They'd grab Shawn, too, if they had to. Maine would be livid if they let Brian slip away.

But they didn't have to.

After Brian had disappeared into the elevator, after Shawn had left the hotel, the three men casually made their way up to Brian's room. With one quick phone call, Frankie had gotten his room number from the desk clerk on their way over; he'd claimed he was a cop and had the experience to sound legit. Only a minimal amount of intimidation had been necessary. They didn't want the police knocking on every room in the hotel, alarming their guests, did they?

Now, outside of Brian's door, it was Crow's turn to go to work. Years ago, for occasions like these, he had stolen a Hilton keycard, modified it, and wired it to a small black box of his own design. The box had numerous buttons and lights on it. It was essentially a simplified code breaker. Since most hotel keycards were nearly identical in size, he could make it work just about anywhere.

He removed the device from his briefcase and slid the keycard into the slot on Brian's door. Two six-inch wires ran from the modified card to the black box. He pressed a series of buttons. A red light began to flash. On the digital display, glowing green numbers scrolled through combinations too fast to read. They stopped. The red light blinked off. A bright green light just above it came on. The lock clicked.

~

They weren't watching me, Brian told himself, lying in bed, eyes closed. *They were just hotel guests.*

His door opened fast. Light from the hall shot across the multicolored carpet. He tried to turn over in bed, to get a look at the intruders, but barely saw the three men in suits sweep in before one had a knee in his back. They moved with the speed of demons.

Handcuffs locked around his wrists.

The man with shaggy blond hair opened a briefcase and removed a roll of duct tape. He tore off a piece, which he handed to the man with the crew cut. The crew cut sealed the tape over Brian's mouth while the bald man found the bottle of pills and stuffed it into his coat pocket. Without bothering to dress him, they yanked Brian to his feet and led him out of the room.

He kicked wildly to no avail. His muffled screams dissipated to nothing only feet away.

They escorted him down the hall into the stairwell before they heard a guest open up a door behind them, but they were safely out of sight by then.

On the landing, the crew cut grabbed Brian by the feet while the bald man held him around the chest.

They carried him quickly down four flights, came out into the parking garage. A black van was waiting right outside the door.

They shoved Brian into the back. Two of the men climbed in there with him. The third took the driver's seat.

As late as it was, there was no parking attendant to watch the exit. The wooden arms were raised.

They pulled into traffic, made several sharp turns.

Brian squealed and fought against the knee in his back, even though he knew it was too late to escape. The bald man removed a gun from underneath his blazer. He held it close enough to the floor so that Brian could see it.

Brian stopped squirming. Instead, he looked up through the tinted windows at the dark sky above. What had happened to his life?

~

Another turn. Another parking garage. Another elevator. As nondescript as all of it was, he had seen this garage, this elevator enough times to recognize them. He was back at Omega.

The bald man inserted a key into a small hole at the base of the keypad and they dropped . . . one floor? Two? Brian couldn't be sure. No matter how many floors it was, though, Brian was surprised to find them going down. Until now, he had believed this elevator could only go up from this floor.

When the doors opened, his kidnappers dragged him down a long white hallway that he had never seen before.

At the end of the hallway was another door. The bald man typed in a code on the adjacent keypad. Like on Crow's homemade code breaker, a red light turned green, permitting access. They took him inside.

Here, the floor was covered with thin gray carpet. Strange machinery crowded the room. A deprivation tank. An electric chair. A slanted steel table with attached leather straps. Something that looked like a cage barely big enough for a person. A long wooden box that reminded Brian of a coffin.

Tall bookshelves full of pill bottles and an untold number of caged rats accented the horrific décor.

Standing dead center in this terrifying space was Mr. Maine. The twitching, stuttering Steven was slightly behind him.

The crew cut and the bald man held him tightly while shaggy closed the door. Then Maine nodded and the bald man ripped the tape off Brian's mouth.

Although he wanted to scream for help, shock kept him silent. Besides, he knew it wouldn't do any good.

The bald man handed Maine the bottle of pills he'd taken from the hotel room. The CEO frowned at them. He passed the bottle to Steven.

"There's a lot of them missing," Steven said.

Maine disregarded the comment. Instead, he looked directly at Brian and asked, "What do you remember?"

Brian breathed through his mouth, trying not to smell the decay, sulfur, and iodine that seemed to hang in the air. Fear held his tongue.

"Do you remember where you're from?"

Finally, he managed a hoarse whisper. "Why shouldn't I?"

Maine flinched as if he had been struck. Steven crossed his arms and clenched his jaw. "You remember your name?" Maine asked.

"Brian."

Maine leaned forward to better hear the young man. "What?"

"Brian Dore."

He smiled a weird, unnatural smile. "That's right. So,

tell me, Brian Dore, how you know about this room. How did you get in here?"

"I've never been here before."

Speaking to Brian as if he were a child, Maine said, "It's not good to lie. We've got you on tape."

"What are you talking about?"

Steven shook the bottle in his hand. "What d-d-did you want with these?"

"I don't even know what they are."

"We could have done so much worse before, Brian. We spared you. This is how you repay us?" Maine asked.

"Please, Mr. Maine," Brian said, confused not only by the entire situation, but by Maine's choice of words, as well. "I really don't know what you're talking about."

The girl, the notes. . . .

"Two days ago everything made sense. Everything was exactly like it was supposed to be."

The pills, the dream. . . .

"Then someone broke in and killed the man who raised me."

The blood dripping down the wall. . . .

A tear formed in one eye and rolled down Brian's cheek. "I don't understand anything anymore." He just kept hoping—especially now—that he could go back to sleep and wake up Monday morning to find out this was all a dream. "The pills," he continued, "somebody left them for me. I don't know who. I swear, I didn't know they were Omega's. I don't even know what they are."

"I told you not to lie," Maine said. "Jerry told everyone about them."

The Diaxium.

"Like I said, we have you on tape." He stepped to the side and Steven followed his lead. Brian could now clearly see the long wooden table behind where they had been standing. On it sat a small monitor sandwiched between two humming computers. Maine took control of the mouse. He quickly navigated his way through a series of screens to a virtual control panel. He clicked on the PLAY button. "Sunday night," he said as the black screen above the control panel came to life.

Brian watched, horrified and confused, as he saw himself move down the white hallway, dressed in just a lab coat, carrying the pills. The only explanation he could imagine, as unlikely as it seemed, was that at some point, during his thirty-hour sleep, he'd executed the theft, met Raven, twisted her into his dream, and convinced himself the pills had been left at an earlier time.

Such a scenario would explain why the pieces of the day hadn't fit together right.

But he was forced to dismiss it. Not only was it as absurd a theory as any Shawn might come up with, it didn't explain the missing gun. And, most importantly, he didn't know about the room!

He didn't have a key for the elevator or the code for the keypad. He simply couldn't have gotten in. The tape must have been manipulated.

73

Maine stopped the playback and turned off the monitor. "Let's cut through the crap. How many pills have you taken?"

"Just one," Brian said, too scared to lie. The crew cut and the bald man still had a solid grip on him.

"Th-th-there's more than—" Steven pinched his face tight to get the phrase out. "There's more than one missing."

"I swear I only took one."

Maine clasped his hands behind his back and smirked. "Fine, you just took one. What was it like?"

"I had this awful nightmare," Brian said. He sensed that the only way he was going to get out of this situation alive was to tell the truth. "I remember an explosion, crumbling buildings, dirty streets. It all happened so fast. Nobody in the nightmare spoke English, I know that. But I don't know what was going on. It was like they were in the middle of a war."

"Can you be more specific? When the dream started, where were you?"

"I guess it was like . . . like a club."

"What makes you say that?"

"There were flashing lights and music. It just looked like a club."

"Were there people there?"

"Yeah."

"Did any of them notice you when the dream started?"

"Well, they all did," Brian said, nervously.

74

"Did any of them speak to you?"

"There was this one girl. She spoke to me."

"Could you understand her?"

"No. Like I said, she didn't speak English."

"Do you know what language she was speaking?"

Brian thought for a moment, trying to remember her words, the accent. But he couldn't. His mouth went dry. Despite the cool temperature in the lab, sweat dripped down his face. Maybe it was German, he told himself. However, after meeting the girl in the hospital, he no longer trusted his memory of the dream, no matter how clear it seemed. He must have unconsciously changed her appearance, he told himself. And if that were true, what else might he have changed? "No. I can't say for sure. I'm sorry."

"That's okay," Maine said, reassuringly. "You're doing fine."

However, the fatherly tone only made Brian more uneasy about his situation.

"Then what happened?"

"Then there was an explosion."

"Really?"

"Really. The whole wall came crashing down and these guys on motorcycles rode in, shooting up the place. Everyone ran. It was chaos."

"What did you do?"

"The girl. She helped me. She got me out of there."

"Where did you go?"

"Nowhere." Maine looked skeptical, so Brian explained. "I mean, we got out of the club and into the city. Then we ran. We just ran."

"Interesting. This city you dreamed about. What did it look like?"

"I don't know. I didn't really get a good look at it."

"But you must have seen something."

"I guess it was just like any other big city. I swear—I really don't know how to describe it. I didn't see much."

"And then what happened?"

"I woke up."

"What do you mean? You just woke up?"

"Yeah. I just woke up."

With his hands still clasped behind his back, tapping one finger against his pinky ring, Maine considered Brian's story for some time. While he thought, nobody spoke. Eventually, he asked, "That was the only time you've taken a pill?"

"The only time."

Steven raised a finger, opened his mouth, about to protest.

"How would you feel about taking another one?" Maine asked, before Steven could say anything. "Here. In a controlled environment. Where it's safe."

Nothing about Maine's sub-level lab looked safe to Brian.

"We need to know more about that dream world you wandered into," Maine continued. "It's important . . . for our research."

"But the dream probably won't be the same," Brian said.

"Don't worry yourself about that. As long as you tell us the details of the dream, it doesn't matter what you dream about."

Brian, who had already been trembling, began to feel the vibrations in his legs. He was trapped. His boss was about to experiment on him as if he were one of the rats.

Maine told Steven to get a cup of water and Steven disappeared behind another door.

"Just one time," Maine told Brian in Steven's absence. "Just take one more pill. If you tell us everything when you wake up, every detail, all will be forgiven."

Brian said nothing. Steven returned with a cup of water. He gave it to Maine and took one of the pills from the bottle the bald man had handed over. After he gave that to Maine, too, the CEO moved to within a foot of Brian. "Open your mouth."

Brian trembled, but refused to follow orders.

Maine's eyes shot toward the bald man. "Open his mouth."

Using one hand, the bald man pried Brian's teeth apart. His other hand was locked tightly around Brian's bicep to secure him in place.

Brian wanted to resist, but couldn't. Maine dropped the pill into Brian's mouth and poured the water in after it. Then, without being told, Rock held Brian's mouth shut.

He let go of Brian's bicep to clamp his nose, as well.

Seizing the opportunity, Brian thrashed, trying to get free, but the man with the crew cut still had a solid grip on him. With shaggy standing just a few feet behind him, even if he could escape, he wouldn't get far.

As the lack of oxygen took hold, reflex forced down the pill. Immediately after his Adam's apple bobbed, the bald man allowed him to breathe. One long breath. Several more followed—quick and shallow.

Now he was mad. Before he'd been scared, but now he was mad. He'd been violated—poisoned, for all the difference it made. Locking eyes with Maine, he cursed without restraint while uselessly thrashing about, trying to break loose of the men holding him.

If he could escape and vomit up the pill before—

But he couldn't. When he collapsed to his knees, shivering, heart pounding, the two men holding him let go. He began to convulse. Everything went black. He couldn't know that Maine had no plans of releasing him after his trip. He couldn't know, since he thought he was only passing out, that the men in that room watched him fade into nothing.

His boxers and the handcuffs fell to the floor.

~

Because new dimensions—or, as Lester referred to them, probability chains—spin off every fraction of every second, most spin off at points that would not seem significant in and of themselves. That, on one Saturday afternoon in his favorite coffee shop, Maine ordered an espresso in one probability chain and tea in another was not the kind of thing that made or broke kings.

But over time, the rift that divided those two probability chains would expand. Thousands of years later, Lester figured, they would in some ways still reflect each other, while in others be unrecognizably different.

And Maine was anxious for Brian to return and tell them in detail about the one they had tuned him into.

CHAPTER 10

Lester was right.

Having spun off many, many years ago, the probability chain into which they had tuned Brian was different from his in many ways.

The United States, known simply as the Northern Continent in the alternate probability chain, was divided into fourteen territories, each of which functioned like an independent country. They obeyed their own laws, followed their own leaders.

With eighteen hundred square miles in the central and northern regions largely uninhabitable due to frequent wind storms and flooding, most of these territories had been established along the southern edge of the continent.

The one into which Brian had shifted was called Artubal.

Artubal shared borders with two other territories: Moriba to the north, Orig to the west. To the east and south, the territory extended all the way to the ocean.

Due to the arid landscape that encompassed most of the territory and the horrific creatures that slithered beneath its sand outside of the capital city of Drekar, few of Artubal's citizens lived anywhere else. Of those who did, most lived in towns to the far west and north, beyond the desert's edge.

However, despite its inhospitable terrain, Artubal had been a prized territory for many decades. It was the only one to have coastline along the eastern edge of the continent and had thrived by taxing merchants from outside its borders for the use of its ports. Travel between the surrounding territories and Artubal's coasts was safe as long as merchants stayed on the wide cement roads.

The territory's most distinguishing feature was The Palace, a seventeen-story glass tower, constructed in the shape of an upside-down pyramid. The Palace, which was how citizens referred to both the building and the government, was an engineering marvel. Seeming to defy the laws of gravity, it had been built as a symbol of Artubal's limitless wealth and superiority to all other territories.

But when rumors became reality and a high-speed rail line united the western edge of the Northern Continent with trading partners in the Distant East, the economic state of the territory began to decline.

At first, only sea trade suffered, since many merchants in territories near Artubal still preferred to go to the closer ports. But as the transcontinental rail line extended its reach farther into the continent, fewer and fewer merchants made the journey to Artubal. After all, the merchants figured, the trains moved at an astounding five hundred miles per hour and cost less than shipping by sea.

Ports closed. Coastal towns died off.

Unable to produce any goods of its own, Artubal found itself with more money going out than coming in—and its budget turned upside down. Now, with the territory in a protracted, twelve-year war with Moriba over land, it teetered at the edge of an unrecoverable economic collapse. And Drekar, home to just over two million people, was feeling the pressure.

The emptiness around him gave way to a dark city street. He could hear traffic. A blaring horn. Yet he could do nothing more than roll to his knees while waves of nausea rippled through his body.

Like in his last nightmare, the sky was dark, the city dirty. One palm was pressed into a pool of oil. He vomited while a rusty car slammed on its breaks, stopping inches away.

The vehicle was boxy and small, and had no windshield. Wearing large, round goggles made of thick copper, the driver got out of the car, shouting in a language Brian didn't know.

Ignoring him, Brain looked around. There were people everywhere. Most clothes were black or gray, had tears, needed to be washed, had started to unravel. All sleeves were cut short and collars were too small.

Many of the people drove strange, rusted-out cars. Others weaved through traffic on what might have been elongated motorcycles, like Harleys that had been stretched from the axles. The vehicles choked, sputtered, and spit out gray exhaust.

Both sides of the street were lined with two- and three-story buildings made of something that seemed to be bumpy cement. Boxy in design, all sharp angles and small windows, they were nearly identical from one to the next. The first story of most buildings featured small shops— some open, some closed. Those that were open had flashing neon signs behind their windows and bars in front of them. Those that were closed had been secured with roll-down metal doors.

Before Brian could assess what lay behind the windows on the floors above, he saw men in shiny, black uniforms rushing toward him. The skin-tight rubber shielded them from neck to toe.

On their helmets were two black, circular screens that looked vaguely like headphones. These two devices were joined across the back of the skull by three strips of thin steel. Attached to the strips of steel was a curved piece of bulletproof rubber, designed to protect its wearer from a shot to the back of the head.

All of these men had guns, and all the guns had lights.

The traffic slowed them some, but they were definitely coming.

Brian gathered his senses as quickly as he could. Just before escaping down a narrow alley, he noticed that half the buildings to his left were suddenly plunged into darkness. Every light behind every window went out. Every neon sign stopped flashing.

He wanted to go home. He cursed Maine for making him take the pill, turned into an alley that was slightly more spacious, and saw something that he assumed must be a garbage bin.

With the men pursuing him back there somewhere, he decided it would be his best place to hide.

He struggled with the handle. A small panel on the side slid open. Flies buzzed out and the inside stank of rotting meat. Dead flesh.

With the interior shrouded in darkness, he scampered through the hole headfirst. He landed and the contents beneath him settled ever so slightly. From inside the cold plastic bags underneath him, something cracked.

The panel he'd opened from outside was even harder to close from the inside. But once it was closed, he decided he was safe. The best thing to do for now was to wait.

Flies settled in his hair and on his skin. Leaning against one wall, he balanced himself precariously on the garbage underneath.

He waited. He listened.

As he rocked unsteadily, something scratched the bottom of one naked foot.

He stooped to remove the nail or glass or whatever it was and found instead a fingernail. Attached to a finger. Attached to a hand. Sticking out of some sort of plastic bag.

He was standing on corpses! Decaying, cold corpses.

Was this how the dead were treated here? Not buried, but discarded?

He wanted to scream. He wanted to escape. But there were footsteps. The men in their shiny, black uniforms with their shiny, black guns. And as certain as he was that he could survive a death in this make-believe world, he didn't want to take any chances.

What if this is one of those dreams where if you die, you don't wake up? Hadn't he heard that somewhere?

He wasn't thinking rationally anymore.

What if, instead of killing him, they meant to imprison him, or *torture* him? After all, they wouldn't be coming with guns if they were coming to help. He'd already been here longer than he had on his last visit. There was no telling what sort of pain they might inflict before the drug wore off.

If he woke up.

A passing thought followed, whispering behind his more prevalent worries: *The world in this dream seems identical to the last.* But another thought answered: *Since he had been discussing this dream world only moments before passing out, it makes sense that he had returned to it.*

However, if this world was his creation—which it was—maybe he could escape to a different world.

He closed his eyes, shutting the darkness out to focus on the light within.

He tried to picture someplace beautiful, with flowers, green grass, and waterfalls. Somewhere relaxing. Somewhere nice. Instead, his imagination drifted back to his junior year in high school, where he'd spent seven months dating the beautiful and smart Alicia Forbs. Alicia had planned to get a degree in political science, but ultimately had her eye on a law degree and a career in Washington. She had long, blond hair, green eyes, and freckles on her cheeks. Two weeks after they'd met in English class, they'd become inseparable. Most weekends between March and May, they'd taken to walking hand in hand through Piedmont Park, where they would discuss the things they'd read, problems at school, and the kind of nothing that filled most conversations between young lovers, the kind of nothing where you talk for hours and then can't remember what you talked about for so long.

When Alicia was offered a scholarship to George Washington University in DC, Brian encouraged her to go. They promised to stay in touch. She promised to see him soon. But inevitably they drifted apart and eventually agreed there was no reason to carry on as a couple. Their lives had gone in different directions and there was no telling when they might align again.

While the last moments of any relationship can be heartbreaking, Brian was thankful that it hadn't ended under worse circumstances. Had it ended with an affair, the separation would have been much more devastating, he told himself. However, as it was his only long-term relationship to date, he had nothing to which he could compare it.

Concentrating on those weekend walks, he tried to see the park, to feel Alicia's hand in his, to smell the spring air. He tried to remember her smile. He tried to recount their conversations.

He concentrated on these memories until he was certain that he must have transformed his dream world, only to open his eyes and find himself still in the dark, stinky garbage bin.

That's when he knew he couldn't escape by simply imagining himself somewhere else. He was stuck until the drug ran its course.

With these corpses.

Lovely.

Strange words were shouted from somewhere in the alley and the footsteps faded.

Still rocking on the bodies, breathing through his mouth, Brian could think of only two options. He could stay here, wait for the drug to pass—tolerate the flies and the stench, risk having corpses thrown on top of him—or he could search for discarded clothes among the bodies and try to meander through the city like he belonged. Then a thought occurred to him: *If I'm dreaming of the same place I dreamed of last time, maybe I can find that girl.*

She had helped him before. She might help him again.

He decided to seek her out because at least it gave him something to do. He slowly worked his way onto all fours and ripped open the bags on top. He shooed away the flies and praised the darkness for hiding the details of the bodies. There was no telling how much flesh decay had already claimed.

None of this is real.

Against the back wall he found a body that was dressed rather than bagged. It was the only one. From all the others, the clothes had been stripped. Perhaps this man had been discarded by loved ones who couldn't imagine robbing him of his dignity by leaving him naked.

Brian worked the garments off the body, only letting the stench of rotting flesh into his nose once. But once was enough. Everything inside him twisted. It took all of his will not to vomit again.

After he finished undressing the corpse, he fought with the sliding door until it opened. He threw out the clothes and scrambled back onto the street.

As he hoped, there was no one around. He dressed quickly in the dark blue pants and brown shirt. The clothes carried the smell of death. The pants barely stayed up.

As casually as he could, still barefoot, he returned to the main street and tried to blend in.

The uniformed men had all but disappeared. He didn't know where they had come from or where they had gone, but he was glad to see only one, far away on the other side of the road.

He hurried off in the opposite direction. Certainly, they weren't looking for *him,* he decided. They'd been drawn by the uproar. Still, why take any chances?

He moved through the thick crowd and coughed from the exhaust. Dressed in the dead man's clothes, he looked like everyone else. Except for the lack of shoes—and not everyone was wearing shoes—he was comfortable with the disguise.

He walked down streets of varying traffic. Overhead, he heard a helicopter thump past in the distance, but forgot it as soon as it was gone. Small dirty stores with flickering lights and names he couldn't read lined both sides of the road. Like he'd seen when he arrived, most had bars on their windows and gates to lock when closed.

Then he saw something he did recognize: the club. Or the cracked wreckage that used to be a club.

He walked its perimeter until he found the grate he had been led out of before. He retraced his steps down the alleys he had run. He found the building the woman had been pointing to.

When he was nearly close enough to see it had been boarded up, one of those odd-shaped Harleys rolled past and the driver tossed a bottle over his shoulder.

Although Brain could tell it wasn't aimed at him, the shattering glass reminded him of the explosion at the club and made his heart skip.

Inconspicuously as he could, he checked the boarded doors and windows for signs of a way in. Though it had started to rot, the wood was not loose.

Then he remembered the exit the girl had used to lead

him out of the club—a hole hidden by a liquor cabinet. The entrance to this building could be just as hard to find. Thinking about all the James Bond films he'd seen and murder-mysteries he'd read, he started pressing odd-looking bricks, as if one would open up a wall. He passed over grates that blew cold air, unsuccessfully tried to pry them open. When people passed by, he strolled in no particular direction until they were out of sight. He moved around to the back of the building where more brick walls hid him from view. He pressed other bricks, fingered holes, and pulled at loose stones.

He was beginning to feel stupid.

He was ready to give up, to wander on, when a grate underneath him collapsed. He fell into a square, cement tunnel. He landed on his side, hands out, and groaned. His hip ached and his palms burned. Above him, the grate, which hung by only one hinge, creaked as it swung itself shut.

Before he could realize what was happening, a group of dark figures swooped him up and carried him away.

The figure in front navigated the square, cement tunnel with a flashlight. Keeping its tiny, narrow beam aimed at the damp ground, they moved swiftly around corners, through a blue, swirling fog.

Uselessly, much like with the men who had kidnapped him earlier, he fought their grip. When he screamed, a hand covered his mouth. When he bit a finger, they chattered to each other in their foreign tongue. Then they dropped him to his stomach and one of them used his fist to deliver a blow squarely to the base of Brian's skull.

Pain shot down his spine just before he lost consciousness.

~

Dressed in heavy clothing, the dark figures carried Brian through more than a mile of tunnels. These cement tunnels and the grates to which they led had been built many years ago when the territory could see no end to its wealth. They were The Palace's solution to the unbearably hot summer months, during which pedestrians often suffered from heat strokes and dehydration. Although above ground they were nothing more than vents where one could stand to cool off for a moment, their development had received tremendous praise from Drekar's citizens. Since then, though, the mechanisms that automatically shut off the system when it wasn't needed had broken and cool air now pumped through the tunnels at all hours.

When the dark figures reached their exit, it did not take them back to the surface. Rather, it was a crudely carved hole on the west side of the tunnel that opened onto miles of hand-dug passageways.

Those passageways, which let to other tunnels and other buildings, formed an extensive network underneath large portions of the city.

As they traveled, they passed men and women, dressed in furry, thick coats, working with pickaxes and shovels to clear new routes.

~

When Brian finally awoke, he was leaning against a brick wall on a dirty tile floor, unsure whether this was the same dream.

His vision cleared. A fire in the middle of the room illuminated a rectangular hole in the floor in a far corner, an open doorway, and a staircase that had been sealed off by rubble.

Huddled around the fire were men and women dressed much like those he had seen on the street.

As he spun his head to get a better look at the room, he saw that every wall was lined with bookshelves. Every bookshelf was home to as many cobwebs as books.

One of the women near the fire finally noticed his eyes were open. With long blond hair that had started to matt into dreadlocks, wearing a mud-stained, yellow tee shirt and wool pants, she came close and said something he couldn't understand.

Brian's brow furrowed with confusion. "Huh?"

Then she shouted over her shoulder and a skinny, middle-aged man appeared in the doorway. He had long, pale cheeks and thinning, gray hair that almost touched his shoulders. His coat, which appeared to be made of brown fur, possibly wolf fur, largely concealed the thread-thin, white button-down he wore underneath it; unlike the button-down shirts in Brian's real world, though, this one buttoned from neck to hip and had no collar. His brown pants, which were tucked into a pair of black work boots, were made of something akin to burlap.

Behind him followed a young woman.

When they got closer, Brian recognized the young woman as Raven. Once again, she was dressed in black, leather pants that had a rip down one thigh, and knee-high, leather boots. Underneath a jacket that was also made of black leather, she had on an aging, purple blouse with numerous stains of undeterminable origin.

The woman who had approached previously stepped back to make room for the middle-aged man and . . . his daughter? Maybe?

They kneeled in front of him.

As Brian watched them speak to each other in a language as foreign to him as Chinese, fear settled in. Everything smelled real. His body still ached from the fall. His neck still throbbed from the jab. His head pounded. He could feel the grime on his skin. Worst of all, try as he might, he hadn't been able to change his fantasy or wake up.

Was he stuck here? Stuck in this dream world forever?

The young woman tenderly pulled Brian's right hand toward her. She turned it over, like she had done at the club, and ran two fingers along the back, from wrist to knuckles. She said something in her strange tongue, and the older man grunted in agreement.

Afterward, she said several things in Brian's direction that sounded like questions. Finally, pointing to herself, she said, "Raivine."

The way she pronounced her name sounded like "Ry-veen."

Brian likewise told her his name.

She hesitantly smiled. They had made a connection. She turned to the man beside her—

~

—"I think he's harmless," Raivine Narva said to her father, still kneeling on the floor in front of Brian.

"But you don't know. We don't know where he came from or why he's here," Axle responded.

Axle Narva was the leader of The Resistance, a group of more than four hundred men and women who believed the territory's current ruler, Leon Chricton, was responsible for the decaying state of their economy, their cities, their lives.

And they had good reason to believe as much.

As the territory choked in the vice of a dwindling revenue stream, Leon tried to manage Artubal's losses by cutting jobs across that were Palace-funded.

Eight years later, with the reduced spending from The Palace rippling through the economy, many small businesses had shut down. Those that survived had done so by selling an assortment of goods, well beyond their original line, and weren't above bartering when a customer had something of value to trade. Due to this hodgepodge, most storefront businesses now resembled consignment shops and thrift stores. To protect the small slice of the economy they had managed to hold onto, the owners invested in rolling steel doors and bars for their windows. The territory's economy appeared to be in an unrecoverable tailspin. Unemployment had reached a staggering twenty-five percent and Leon's popularity was at an all-time low.

Desperate not to go down in history as the man who had undone all the progress made under his father's rule, Axle believed, Leon made an announcement that shocked everyone. Broadcasted over the radio and in massive larger-than-life images on each of The Palace's glass walls, he said he had recently learned that their trusted ally Moriba was actually the largest financial contributor to the rail line project, and that they had done so to cripple Artubal and assume the territory when it fell.

"I will not let that happen!" His greasy, black hair was slicked back from his oval face and he was wearing a pressed, bright-red coat that buttoned to the collar. His big nose looked excessively large at this size and his pale skin seemed to glow. Across the drab, gray city, his massive image was in such contrast that he almost looked godlike. "We will fight back. They will not take our land. We will take theirs!"

A roar of applause rose from the city.

"Never fear. Prosperous times lie ahead," he said over the roar.

Then he offered jobs to any men and women over the age of sixteen who wished to join the Enforcers. The Enforcers acted as both the military and police force for the territory.

But the truth, according to Axle, was that Moriba had contributed nothing to the rail line, had no intentions of taking over Artubal, and that Leon had only made those claims to obtain the support of the territory for his own war plans. If he could assume control of Moriba, he would get with it its many square miles of usable farmland as well as a significant number of production factories, which would breathe new life into Artubal's economy.

At the time of the announcement, Axle had already doubted Leon's ability to lead. His unconventional method of cutting the crime rate years before had left him uneasy; it had been an unprecedented overreach of authority, an invasion of privacy. Nonetheless, he had stood in solidarity with the citizens of Artubal in support of the war. *Whatever it took to survive,* he had said.

Later, he would regret not organizing The Resistance on the very day the announcement was made. But it wasn't until the war shattered his own small universe that he would decide something had to be done.

When The Palace's actions took from him what he

valued most, he decided that without question Leon Chricton could not remain in power. He had cost the territory too much. He had cost Axle too much.

Quickly he learned he was not the only one who felt this way. And once The Resistance agreed that the territories should unite, but under Moriba's rule, the organization found its purpose. It was not about reform, but revolution.

Although overwhelmed and afraid eleven years ago when they had first fled the city above, the members of The Resistance were now highly organized.

The adults worked in shifts to clear new tunnels beneath the city. Most of their remaining time was occupied by weapons training, target practice, hand-to-hand combat drills, and studying military strategy.

The children, grouped by age, were educated in the basement of an abandoned school building. They were taught history, mathematics, science, and literature. Their parents, all members of The Resistance, had decided long ago that only those children who insisted on training with the adults would do so, and only after they'd turned sixteen.

Unfortunately for Axle, Raivine had been one of those to insist. Now, after years of training, she was probably as tough as anybody else in their movement. She was certainly as smart. But that didn't mean he would trust her judgment over his own when it came to strangers.

"Look at him," Raivine said. "He's scared. He's

confused. He doesn't even speak our language. What danger could he be?"

"So he pretends."

"Axle," Raivine said, scolding him. Rarely did she call him by name. "Father" was what he preferred. "Father" was what was appropriate. But when she got irritated or angry, she abandoned tradition and addressed him as an equal.

"Perhaps he's like the robed one," Axle responded, "the one we've heard stories about lately. The one who speaks two languages—both a foreign tongue and our own."

"I told you, it's been a month since I've seen this man."

"That's when the stories began. Maybe they came together."

Brian said something neither could understand, and the two halted their conversation long enough to throw a glance in his direction.

Then Raivine turned her attention back to her father. "You're being ridiculous." She reached a hand out to Brian, which he cautiously took, and helped him to his feet.

"What are you doing?"

"I'm taking him into our chambers, Father. He'll feel safer there, without so many strangers around."

Axle clenched his fists, ready to say something he'd regret, when she added, "He needs our help, Father."

CHAPTER 11

The basement of the library had been named the Haven. It was the first place The Resistance had taken refuge when forced underground and, thanks to its direct access to the ventilation shafts, had been the starting point for their underground network.

Raivine and Brian were barely on the other side of the door when two hands appeared through the rectangular hole in the floor that connected the basement to those ventilation shafts. Up came a man dressed in ragged pants, scuffed shoes, and an orange, long-sleeved shirt with a tear down one arm. He was out of breath and frantic, and everyone noticed.

His name was Noor Zata. He was wiry and lean. His shaggy blond hair stuck out in every direction, stiff as straw. He'd been with The Resistance since the beginning. Although his nerves were often frayed, his patience regularly thin, his movements sudden and jerky, no one had ever seen him like this.

He ran over to Axle. "You're here. Good. I'm so glad you're here."

"What is it, Noor? What's wrong?"

Noor took several deep breaths before continuing. "They took the Den."

The Den, a well-guarded secret within The Resistance, was where Axle and his rebels stockpiled their weapons. "You must be mistaken."

Noor shook his head. "I saw it with my own eyes. There's nothing left."

Immediately, Axle called for one of the men and one of the women by the fire—Barat and Sherri—to accompany him as he charged toward the hole.

With Noor trailing, the four slipped into the ventilation shaft beneath the library. Axle turned on a flashlight. "Didn't we have a guard posted?" he asked, as they moved through a hole that led them into tunnels of gray stone and yellowish-brown dirt.

"Two," Noor said.

"And?"

"They're dead. They didn't have a chance. Never had a chance. A troop of Enforcers killed them before they could warn us. They took everything."

~

Raivine's quarters were illuminated by the soft, warm glow of a dozen scattered candles.

"I'm sorry about Father," she said.

Brian slowly lowered himself onto one of the many

pillows that were spread across the black-and-white tile floor.

"He's still a little mad because I was at The Fountain the night of the explosion. You know, the club where I found you. He always called it a high-risk location, partly because we couldn't get there through tunnels. Not all the way, I mean. He keeps telling me how lucky I was that I didn't get killed." She sat down on a pillow across from him and stopped talking. Since he couldn't understand a word she was saying, there was little reason to ramble. If she wanted to have a conversation with him, if she wanted to find out where he was from, they'd have to break the language barrier.

She noticed Brian's gaze slowly follow the stone column in the east corner the twenty feet from floor to ceiling. Each corner had one, and into each column was carved an assortment of geometric shapes. Between them, overflowing bookshelves lined the walls.

Understanding that the vastness of the room might be intimidating, she took Brian's hands into her own, hoping to make him feel safe. Doing so brought him back to her.

"Yes," he said. He nodded, then repeated her name back to her.

Yes. Raivine understood the word by its context. In her language, its equivalent was *sant*. To show that she'd caught its meaning, she nodded and said the word back to him.

For a moment, she saw hope flicker in his eyes. Hope

101

of communication. Hope of understanding.

Nodding again, she said, "Yes. . . . *Sant*."

It was Brian's turn to learn a new word. "*Sant*."

She giggled at his pronunciation.

Excited, he pointed to her and said, "You Raivine." He pointed to himself. "Me Brian."

"You Brian. Me Raivine."

Two more words. She giggled again. It was suddenly clear that, given a little time, they could communicate.

~

Before the Den had been claimed by The Resistance, it had been the basement of a bus terminal.

Although not among the earliest casualties of budget cuts, public transportation had eventually suffered the same fate as so many other services supported by The Palace. At first, the cuts to public transportation affected only a small percentage of bus drivers as less-popular routes were abolished and the frequency of stops on more-popular routes was decreased.

But when Chricton further cut back on funding to pay for his ongoing war with Moriba, the transit system began suffering more serious blows than route reduction. Busses broke down, never to be repaired. Unpaid drivers walked off the job. Finally, after a year in the red, the transit system closed its doors permanently.

When Axle had claimed this building for The

Resistance, he'd done so with only Noor's assistance.

Noor, who'd been among the first drivers fired, was happy to participate.

Following Axle's instructions, they used explosives to collapse the lobby and seal off the entrance to the lower levels. Even if the Enforcers knew The Resistance had chosen this place to hide weapons, moving the rubble above would take time and be noisy. With quick work, The Resistance should have easily been able to relocate the stockpile Moriba had quietly funneled to them and destroy the hole that bridged their tunnels to the basement before anybody could get inside.

Or so Axle believed.

When they reached the hole he had blown into the basement wall, the rocky tunnel gave way to cinderblock and a jagged entrance large enough to walk through.

Axle stopped.

In the faint orange glow of his flashlight lay two dead men, dressed in dirty, gray cotton shirts and muddy slacks. The guards. They were sprawled out on the ground and had been stripped of their weapons. Surprisingly, neither showed any signs of struggle. No fresh wounds. It was as if they'd just collapsed.

"How could this happen?" he asked.

With a stride more urgent than before, he led his crew into the Den. As he'd been told, the debris which blocked access to the basement stairwell had been cleared. The weapons were gone. Except for some old station supplies and deflated tires, there was nothing.

"I told you," Noor said. "It's all gone. Everything."

Axle pulled a gun from underneath his coat as he made a circular motion with one finger. The team, who had also pulled guns, spread out into the darkest corners.

"West side clear."

"South side clear."

"I'm good over here," Noor said.

Without a word from Axle, the four moved toward the center of the room. From there, Axle had a good view of the stairwell. Though he didn't watch it directly while they were talking, he kept it in his peripheral vision.

Any sound or flicker of light from that direction could mean trouble.

"Find anything usable?" he asked all three.

A deflated "No" from all.

Axle sighed. "That's it, then. Except for the weapons in the training cavern and any our members may have on them, there's nothing left. We'll have to start over. We'll have to get word to Moriba." He glanced from one comrade to the other. "However, before we start rebuilding, we have to address the more important problem. Clearly, we have a traitor."

"How do you know?"

"Take a look at the men outside when we leave. Noor, did you actually see the Enforcers kill them?"

"No. I mean, how could I? I just assumed—"

"Exactly. Because if you'd seen them, they would

104

have seen you. And you'd be dead, also."

"But what makes you think there's a traitor? Just because I didn't see it—"

"There are no exterior wounds to the bodies and the guards are still at their posts. If they'd been killed by Enforcers, they would have been shot or stabbed. They would have had time to warn us. And they more than likely would have died in the basement, itself, during combat.

"But," Axle continued, "if they died before the robbery—if they were gassed or poisoned—they wouldn't have had a chance to do anything. They'd still be at their posts, exactly where they are."

"That makes sense," Sherri said.

"Barat, go find a crew to help you seal up this hole and collapse the tunnel," Axle instructed. He pulled out a small, glass canister from the pocket of his coat. In it floated a translucent green liquid. "Take this. It's the last explosive I have. Until we can get more supplies from sympathizers, I can't make any more. Use it wisely."

The sympathizers were residents of the city above who would donate food, clothing, and other supplies to The Resistance, as well as import weapons and transport messages between the rebels and Moriba.

Then Axle turned to Sherri and Noor. "You two get the bodies over to Dr. Shirgarmo's. I want to know exactly what killed them."

Shirgarmo was one such sympathizer. He was, in fact,

the first sympathizer. As a medical professional, he diagnosed illnesses, distributed medicine, and performed minor surgery. But he had never been asked to do an autopsy.

~

Sherri and Noor moved back through the tunnels to a nearby supply closet, which was little more than a hole in the earth with a wooden panel shoved in front of it. They removed the panel and, from the closet, a smaller slab of wood with handles on each end.

"You think we can get them both on here?" Sherri asked.

"Shouldn't be a problem."

With Sherri carrying the wooden slab from the front, they headed back toward the Den. They were silent for most of the walk. Finally, Noor said, "So why'd you join The Resistance?"

"Same reasons you did, I suppose. To take The Palace. To make life livable again."

"You think it was ever really livable?"

"Every life has its problems. But, come on. Hell, you should know. You know how things used to be. This isn't the way I grew up."

"It could be worse."

Sherri stopped and turned, and Noor fell into his step. "Things could be worse? That's okay with you?"

"I'm just saying, look on the bright side."

Irritated, she pushed her hair away from her face. "Come on, we have to get to Dr. Shirgarmo."

Then she turned back around, lifted one handle onto her shoulder, and kept walking. After a while, she asked, "Why did you join?"

"Same reason, I suppose."

"No, really. If you think things could be worse, why are you here? You were a bus driver. I would think if anybody should be mad, it should be you. You lost your job, your livelihood. Just like all the others. You really think things could be worse?"

"All I meant was, at least we're alive. . . . It could be worse."

Sherri sighed. "Sometimes I'm not so sure."

When they reached the Den, they dragged the bodies onto the wooden slab. They were heavy and cumbersome and, as it turned out, the board was too narrow to fit both bodies on it side by side—one had to be partially draped across the other to move them both in one trip.

Before lifting the slab, Sherri closed both sets of eyelids. As many corpses as she had seen, the eyes of the dead shouldn't bother her anymore. But they still did. She felt like she could see in them fear, horror, anger, sadness—whatever emotion had last possessed them.

"Ready? Up."

They lifted the slab and carried the bodies through the rocky tunnels and the cold cement passageways to a fake wall that led them into the basement of Dr. Shirgarmo's office.

Shirgarmo, who now lived in that basement, awoke from the rumble of the door as it slid forward and to the side. The door, designed by The Resistance, had been built of artificial cinderblocks (much lighter than their original counterparts) and steel runners. Twice now, Enforcers had overlooked it while inspecting his office.

In the basement, he kept a small bed, a dresser, a desk, and a fold-out table. One corner had been converted into a makeshift kitchen.

Before the door had opened all the way, he was on his feet, alert and jittery. He was nearing seventy, but moved quickly for his age. Hands covered with liver spots tied a bathrobe around his waist. Wiry gray hair stuck out from the sides of his head. He slouched and the skin under his chin sagged some.

"Oh, my," he said, as Sherri and Noor brought the bodies in. "Oh, my. This is terrible. This is—What is this?"

With a grunt from Noor, they put the slab on the ground. Then Noor slid the door behind them back into place.

"We need you to tell us what killed them," Sherri said.

"You've never—"

"I know. We've never asked you to do an autopsy before. This is different." She hesitated. "We think we might have a traitor."

Twitching fingers played around the doctor's chin and drummed the side of his cheek. His eyes stayed on the bodies. "A traitor. Hmm. A traitor."

"If you don't think you can do this," Noor started to say, but Shirgarmo wasn't listening.

"A traitor, hmm." He knelt and dragged the second body off the first so that he was looking at the front of both. He felt their skulls, twisted their heads. "No signs of bludgeoning. No." He checked for blood on their clothes. "No external wounds."

"How long will this take?" Noor asked.

For the first time since the bodies had been placed on the floor, Shirgarmo looked up. "This could take some time. Yes, indeed. This could take some time. Blood work might be needed. And maybe other tests."

"How long?"

"Time." He nodded toward some wooden stairs. "I have a table in my office. Take them up there."

"What if the Enforcers come back?" Sherri asked. "We obviously don't want them to know you're working with us."

"That's sweet," he said. "You're a sweet girl. They were just here yesterday. They won't be back anytime soon." He stepped away from the bodies. "Take them upstairs."

CHAPTER 12

Raivine and Brian quickly taught each other more words: pillow, candle, floor, ceiling, wall, door. But in her small quarters, there were a limited number of nouns they could refer to. Raivine ran a finger along her arm. "*Frata.*"

"Arm," Brian said.

She repeated the word and then placed the same finger against her cheek. "Arm."

Although Brian wanted to laugh, he resisted the urge because he knew she was being serious. "No," he said, and she looked confused. A moment later, he understood why. He touched her cheek. "Skin." Her arm. "Skin." His arm. "Skin."

She smiled. "*Frata.* Skin."

"Yes. *Frata* is skin."

"Is? . . . *Frata* is skin." Her eyes lit up. "I is Raivine. You is Brian."

Close enough, Brian thought. He was impressed by the speed at which she was soaking up his language.

Then the door burst open. . . .

~

Axle stormed inside. He passed his daughter and grabbed Brian by his shirt. Then, while dropping to one knee, he shoved Brian onto his back. "Tell me who you are right now! Tell me who you are right now, or I swear . . ."

He pulled a knife from a sheath in his boot. Its handle was wooden, intricately carved into the shape of a human body standing erect. The blade was six inches long.

"Father! What are you doing?" Raivine was suddenly on her feet, but still keeping some distance.

"Stay out of this."

Brian started babbling, and Raivine caught only a few words—nothing that made any sense with her limited vocabulary.

"This is crazy; who do you think he is?" Raivine demanded.

"Maybe he's the robed one. The one who speaks two languages." To Brian: "Is that who you are?"

But, not understanding Axle's tongue, Brian just stared back at him, wide-eyed with fear.

"Axle, please, stop. Calm down."

"Last time you saw this man was at the club, right?"

"Yeah, so?"

"The night it blew up."

"What's your point?"

"Next time he turned up was today."

"Father, get that knife away from his eyes. You're

111

scaring him."

Moving his gaze from Raivine to Brian, he said to her, "Do you know what happened today?"

"No, I—"

"They took the Den. And guess who was here just in time to keep us distracted. . . ."

"Axle, please put the knife down. I think you're wrong about this."

"I don't think so." He moved the blade close enough to Brian's eye to scoop it out of its socket.

Raivine slammed her boot onto the floor. The candles shook. "Father! Before you hurt him, tell me what you think he did."

Axle glanced at his daughter long enough to see the frustration in her penetrating stare. Her arms tingled with fury. She was as mad as she'd ever been with him. He moved the knife away from Brian's eye, but only a hair— just a twitch of his wrist, and Brian would only have half his sight. "Fine." Then Axle told her in detail about the robbery, the dead guards. "Possibly poison," he said. "Dr. Shirgarmo's checking out the bodies now."

"That has nothing to do with him!"

"Don't be so sure."

"Father, before you do anything rash, hear me out. You started The Resistance for a good reason."

"To save our city," he said.

She hesitated, looking for words. When she found the ones she wanted, she said, "Father, if this robed one really exists, wouldn't it serve us well to have someone on our side who can understand what he's saying when we can't?"

Axle's blade moved another inch from Brian's eye. No one spoke. No one breathed. Finally, he returned the knife to its sheath without answering. "Until we hear from Dr. Shirgarmo, don't let him out of your sight." As he turned to go, he mumbled, "I still don't understand why he never had a chip, no matter which side he's on."

The chip Axle was referring to was officially known as the Honesty Chip. It had been introduced by The Palace within a year of when Leon Chricton assumed leadership of the territory.

At first, more than thirty percent of the population opposed the idea. Of those, though, only a small percentage participated in organized protests against The Palace.

Leon explained that the chip, which was basically a tracking chip, should not be viewed as a way of monitoring or controlling every citizen in the territory, but rather as a way of ensuring their safety. With the chip implanted, criminals could be caught and brought to justice quickly.

To further enforce the idea that this was the intended purpose of the chip, all prisoners held in the Artubal Cells off the coast were ushered through the implantation process first.

But to make sure the Honesty Chip was fully effective,

it could not be limited to those who had already committed crimes. Everyone had to have one. Therefore, he made it mandatory for anybody who sought assistance from The Palace. If you wanted a job anywhere in the territory, you had to have one. If a business was caught employing people without one, it would be shut down. For any new birth, the hospital was required to implant the chip before returning the baby to its mother.

For the first year following the announcement, as people stood in long lines to have the procedure done, as businesses struggled with internal regulations to ensure they were in compliance, the popularity of the new policy dropped even further. People cursed Leon, calling him the worst leader in over a century.

Three years later, though, crime had dropped from seven percent to less than one. The same people who cursed him then praised him for his innovative approach to making the territory safe.

Just a few citizens, men like Axle, who had reluctantly complied with the policy, still felt it was an overreach of power. However, these were still good days, prosperous days, for the territory. It was not the implantation of the Honesty Chip that ultimately led him to form The Resistance. To Axle, in retrospect especially, the chip only marked the beginning of the territory's decline. It was one small piece of a much bigger problem.

Raivine glanced at the back of Brian's right hand as he pushed himself back up. She had also wondered why he

114

had no chip when she first met him. Fingering the scar on her own hand—the one left after her chip had been removed—she reminded herself that he was a foreigner, and that was likely the reason.

She closed the door that Axle had left open. She could tell, even though Brian was once again sitting cross-legged on one of the pillows, that he was uneasy. She could almost hear his heartbeat, feel his tension. She knew what he wanted to know: *Why was that man so angry?*

She sat down in front of him and gently touched his face. "Is OK," she said. "Is OK." Then she nodded, and with her fingers still touching his cheek, she said, "Skin."

CHAPTER 13

The hours passed, and the language lessons were not interrupted again until a stranger with a cropped beard came in to tell Raivine dinner was ready. She thanked him. Once he was gone, she raised a hand to her mouth, opened and closed her jaw to simulate chewing.

"Food?" Brian asked.

"Food." She nodded. "You is . . ." She rubbed her belly, raised her hands, curled her fingers like claws, and growled.

The laughter that had tempted Brian before broke through this time. At first he was ashamed. Then he saw that she was laughing with him. When their laughter subsided, she curled her fingers and growled again; they laughed some more.

"Hungry. Yes, I am hungry."

She stood. "Come," she said, offering a hand to help him up.

She led him into the adjoining room where sixteen people were gathered around the fire. Nearly half of them were roasting rats—skinned and stabbed onto the ends of makeshift skewers.

Raivine found a small opening close to the fire. "Sit," she offered, and he did. Afterward, she turned to the heavyset man beside them. *"Dort dana nectraro, casda."*

He growled back an answer as he shifted his body to shield the two skewers he held. After a brief argument, which ended when she pumped her fist in the air and spat words through gritted teeth, he handed over his second skewer. She passed it to Brian. "Food."

On the skewer he now held, which was actually just a long steel rod with a rubber handle, was a crispy black rodent.

Brian's face twisted with disgust as he imagined biting into the burnt flesh. "No," he said, as he handed the skewer back. "No, thank you." Since this was all a dream anyway, he didn't actually need to eat.

With disappointment, Raivine said, "You hungry."

"No rats." He glanced across the fire to see Axle staring at him. Quickly, Brian looked away.

~

Raven wanted to explain that, while there were over a hundred citizens in the city above who sympathized with their cause, who would donate food when they could, there wasn't always enough to go around. On some days, like today, there wasn't any. And on these days, they made do with whatever they could.

117

Fortunately, for reasons nobody in The Resistance knew, the once-scarce rodent had been seen everywhere lately. She assumed he rejected the food because he wasn't aware of this. She thought he worried that somebody else would go hungry if he accepted the meal. Then she had an idea: Maybe, since he was too considerate to eat the rat, he would eat something that he knew was in greater abundance. She handed the stick of food back to the fat man and told him to save it for her. He reluctantly agreed.

"Come," she said to Brian. She grabbed two coats from a pile and gave him one.

"Where are we going?"

"Get you food." She removed a penlight from her pocket as she led him though the hole in the floor, then used it to light their way as she guided him through the cement ventilation shafts.

~

Brian didn't remember the air being this cold last time he was in the tunnels. Then again, he had spent little time conscious. He rubbed the back of his skull. He could feel a knot forming where he'd been hit. Thankfully, the throbbing headache that had followed was gone.

In the glow of Raivine's penlight, he noticed that the air here was faintly blue. It swirled in on itself, back out and away.

"What are these?" he asked, running one hand along

the wall of the ventilation shaft.

With English still new to Raivine—and Raivine's language completely lost on Brian—the answer took some time. She used the words she had learned and gestured until Brian figured out what she meant. As in her quarters, each time he said a new word, she absorbed it immediately.

By the time they were done, he gathered that the shafts were used—or had been used—to cool pedestrians passing over the vents above. During the daylight hours, the city could be unbearably hot.

"It really gets that hot?"

"Hot, hot, hot." She said it several times to emphasize her point. "People . . ." She mimed a fainting spell, or a death—maybe she meant both—without lifting the light's beam from the ground. "Air cool. People rest."

But since "new power" (to use Raivine's words) had taken control, things had "gone to hell" (to use Brian's). The system was never shut off anymore.

"It's broken," Brian said.

"Broken? No stop?"

"Yes. No stop."

They went through another hole in the cement and through the rocky tunnels her comrades had dug. Soon it opened onto a natural cavern. There, with ceilings so high they disappeared into darkness, giant stalagmites, looming stalactites, and rock formations Brian couldn't identify, the beam from Raivine's penlight glided along an underground field of leafy green plants.

She threw out one arm as if to say "Ta-da!"

~

Sherri watched Dr. Shirgarmo work. The bodies were stretched out along two dented, steel tables. Cabinets, some open, lined the walls of the small lab. A layer of dust and grime was stuck to the blue tile under their feet. Rolls of gauze, pills, and open bottles of various liquids were everywhere. Test tubes lay haphazardly on one long table. Nothing was clean. Nothing was tidy.

In an open brown coat that looked more like a trench coat than one a doctor would wear, Shirgarmo tore into the first body. He used rusty scissors to cut the skin like fabric and a scalpel of sorts for more detailed work. He hovered, quivered with excitement, sipped from an unmarked bottle of liquor. "Hmm, yes, hmm." He scribbled something onto a notepad. With the guts of one victim exposed, he pulled out the intestines with the excitement of a child opening a present.

Sherri watched from a few feet back. She wasn't sure if he knew what he was doing or if this show was for her benefit. He was skilled at diagnosis and prescription, and he'd been an effective surgeon when minor work had been needed, but that didn't make him a coroner.

He put on a pair of glasses that had a telephoto lens attached to one side and peered into the torso of the corpse. He poked the surrounding organs with a finger.

Finally, Sherri folded her arms and asked, "How long is this going to take?"

"Take . . . take . . . time." He grabbed hold of the liver, yanked it out, and dropped it on the ground. "That's not the problem," he mumbled to himself. To Sherri, he said, "Takes time to disassemble a body."

She sighed. "Is all this necessary? After all, we're pretty sure they were poisoned."

He lifted the glasses onto his forehead. "Poisoned. Hmm. Poisoned. Why didn't you say so?" He grabbed a syringe from the table behind him and stabbed it into the victim's arm. When he missed the vein, he stabbed again. "Don't worry, he doesn't feel anything. Nothing at all." To the corpse: "Do you?" He stabbed a third time. "Got it," he said, as he finally drew blood.

Sherri shook her head with frustration as she leaned back against one counter.

Shirgarmo emptied the syringe into a test tube, then placed the test tube on a rack. He gulped down another mouthful of liquor. "Poison or gas?" he asked, wiping the sweat from his brow.

"Weren't you listening? That's why we're here. To find out."

He nodded. "Hmm, right, hmm." He grabbed the scissors, snipped off the end of the corpse's nose, and used tweezers to remove a clump of nose hairs.

~

Brian couldn't understand how plants could grow in complete darkness. Nor did he understand a heat intense enough to justify the ventilation, the bodies discarded in a dumpster, or the language. In fact, the more he learned about his dream world, the less sense it made. The only thing he could get his mind around with any certainty was his attraction to Raivine. If things were different—if she were real . . .

But she was real, wasn't she? Sort of. As long as he was here.

His mind shut off. He lost himself in the tangles of her long dark hair, her silver eyes, soft skin, and kissed her. Gently, briefly, lips closed. When he pulled away, his heart thumped fast with excitement and guilt. *I shouldn't have done that.* It was awkward. Inappropriate. He tensed for the anticipated slap.

But Raivine just smiled, gesturing again toward the field. "Food."

Then a bright flash overtook the cavern.

~

Shirgarmo released the clump of nose hairs into a test tube and filled it halfway with dirty brown water from the tap. Another gulp of liquor. He removed two colorful bottles and two eyedroppers from a cabinet. Into the first test tube, filled with blood, he squirted three drops of something purple. Into the second test tube, with the nose hairs, he squirted three drops of something orange.

He drummed his fingers on the table. More liquor. He wiped his lips with the back of one hand. "Hmm." He returned the colorful bottles and eyedroppers to the cabinet without cleaning them.

Intensely watching the test tubes, he again said, "Hmm."

"What is it?" Sherri asked.

"Oh, nothing. Nothing. This could take a while."

Something scampered across the floor. He turned suddenly and smashed his bare foot down on a roach, grinding it into the tile.

~

A loud crack. A rumble. Brian immediately covered his ears. The flash had left him momentarily blind. With his hands on his ears, he was momentarily deaf, as well.

As soon as he could see again, he looked from Raivine to the field. "What . . ." He followed Raivine's light as she aimed it upward, piercing the darkness above. Now he could see not just the tips of giant stalactites, but gathering storm clouds, as well. They rolled and churned, trapped on all sides by rock.

"That's not possible," Brian said to himself. He realized how foolish his statement was. Since none of it was possible, why shouldn't there be an underground storm?

"Come," Raivine said. "Eat."

Brian nodded, briefly and awkwardly. "OK." Then he followed her down a short incline into the field.

When they were on flat ground again, he realized that the leafy green plants reached almost to his knees. They were taller than he thought, and damp from the drizzle that never stopped.

"Like this," she said, reaching down to grab the bottom of a plant. Before jerking it from the ground, she whispered something to it and gently ran her fingers down its leaves. All the plants nearby seemed to rustle with fear. She gave one strong tug, tearing the plant completely from the earth.

Dirt fell in clumps from its roots. The leaves went limp. Lightning flashed. The plants around her rustled more violently.

"Run!" she shouted.

They weren't yet up the incline when the rain started coming down hard. The clouds above began to circle. The wind picked up. The earth shook. A stalactite crashed down onto the narrow ledge, inches from them and their exit.

Some eight feet in height, it landed on its tip. Fell toward Raivine. Could have crushed her. Brian grabbed her by the waist and dived out of the way.

Later, he would realize that such an act had been more

courageous than he had thought himself capable of. Right now, though, he was too scared for such reflection.

They slid back down the muddy incline, into the rustling plants. The stalactite rolled the other way.

The wind grew stronger and stronger.

Back on her feet, Raivine shoved the penlight into her pocket and clamped the plant between her teeth. Then, in complete darkness, she grabbed Brian's arm. "Follow! Come!" she shouted over the howling storm.

In the flash of lightening that followed, Brian saw her crawling on all fours, fighting the wind, toward the exit. They were both soaked. Her hair whipped her face.

Again in darkness, he heard another stalactite fall. In another flash of lightening, he saw that this one, even larger than its brother, had also rolled away from them.

Terrified, he dug his fingers into the muddy incline and began climbing in the general direction of the exit. Lightening provided sporadic opportunities for him to correct his course and check Raivine's progress.

He fought the wind and rain all the way to the ledge, where he heard another stalactite tear loose. A flash of lightning gave him just enough time to roll out of the way. Grabbing his hand, Raivine dragged him into the adjoining tunnel.

She stopped long enough to hand Brian the plant and turn back on her penlight. "Run!"

At first, Brian didn't understand the urgency of her instructions. He had assumed they were out of danger.

Then he felt the wind on his back, as if the storm were trying to suck them back into the cavern. Thunder cracked loud enough to shake loose rocks from the walls around them, and he did as she had instructed.

~

"Look at that," Shirgarmo said. "Hmm. Look at that." Resting his elbows on the countertop, intensely watching the test tubes, he repeated himself. "Look at that."

Sherri walked up behind him. "What is it?" As soon as she could see over his shoulder, she realized she hadn't needed to ask.

The brownish-yellow chemical with the nose hairs in it twinkled a lime green. The blood hadn't changed color.

"There's your answer," Shirgarmo said.

"They were poisoned."

"Yup, yup, yup. Just like you said they were."

Fixated on the test tube with the nose hairs, Sherri said, "Gas."

"Yup. From the color, I'd bet it was a niaxalate base. Probably *Lyzarda*. Guess that'd make sense, hmm? Can't see it or smell it."

"How fast can it kill you?" Sherri asked.

"Five seconds. Six."

Sherri shook the doctor's quivering hand, thanked him, and ran back down the stairs into his basement. Shirgarmo helped himself to some more liquor as he listened to the fake wall slide open below him. With one last "hmm" he turned his attention back to the test tube. The green twinkle was mesmerizing.

~

Following Raivine's lead, Brian ran. He could feel the storm behind him. Thunder cracking. Lightening flashing. Chasing him. Pulling him. Sucking him back into the cavern.

And then he didn't.

Exactly when he didn't, he couldn't be sure. He was watching Raivine. He was following her, focused on her, focused on the tunnels, focused on the escape.

When they stopped, Brian said, "The storm . . ." With his hands on his knees, he trailed off. He was short of breath. "Now I see why you eat rats."

Raivine wasn't as tired. After two shallow breaths, she took the plant from Brian and tore off a leaf. "Eat this," she said. She put the leaf into her mouth and chewed.

Then she used her finger to draw an imaginary line around the bottom third of the plant. "Never eat below. Death."

She had learned "never," "below," and "death" while they were discussing the ventilation.

She tore off a leaf from the plant and offered it to him. He accepted it, ate it, and found the vegetation—especially the minty aftertaste—to be more pleasant than he had anticipated.

Suddenly, his stomach growled. The acid churned. He needed more.

He devoured the remaining leaves. Neither of them spoke until he was done. After discarding the bottom third, they finished the hike back to the ventilation shafts.

~

Just below the hole that led into the Haven, with its cobweb-covered bookshelves and fire, Raivine raised one finger in the air, telling Brian to stop and to be quiet. Something was wrong. Something had changed. Though she couldn't be sure what, she'd learned never to doubt her intuition. The air felt . . . heavy. That was the closest she could come to describing the feeling.

"Brian," she said, handing him her penlight. "Go back ground tunnel. Wait. Hide. I come."

"Why?"

"Go." She was more forceful this time. He left.

She watched him round a corner, saw the light fade, and waited a little longer. A soft glow from the fire spilled through the hole above her. Once she was sure he was almost there, she pulled herself up into the library.

At first, things looked much as she had left them. The crowd by the fire was laughing, telling stories, making plans for a better tomorrow.

Then she saw Sherri huddled against the far wall with

Axle and Noor. From their faces, she could tell they were involved in an intense discussion. When Sherri finally glanced in her direction, she tapped Axle's shoulder and pointed at his daughter. The three looked over at Raivine.

This was what her intuition warned her about, Raivine realized.

Axle stood and approached. "Where is he?"

"Who?"

"The intruder."

"You mean Brian?"

"I don't care what is his name is. Where is he?"

"Why do you want to know?" She asked this casually, which only made him angrier.

"The guards were gassed."

"So what?"

"Don't make this difficult."

"Father, why can't you trust me on this? He means us no harm."

Axle pushed her wet hair away from her eyes. "What have you been doing?" he asked. When she didn't answer, he added, "You look just like your mother. She would have understood."

"She's dead."

He sighed. She'd only said that to hurt him. Without letting himself get baited into an argument, he calmly said, "This stranger—"

"Brian."

"He's dangerous. Noor and I have discussed it. Please

129

tell us where he is."

She didn't answer.

"You can be very stubborn sometimes, young lady." Turning his back to his daughter, he called Noor and Sherri over.

"Each of you gather a team," he said. "Sherri, you take the west tunnel. Noor and I will go east."

"No, wait," Raivine said. "There's no need for all that. . . . I left him in the east tunnel about two miles down."

Axle smiled. "Thanks, honey." Then he shouted several names. A flurry of activity transpired as six men and women followed Axle through the hole in the floor. Each grabbed a coat from the pile while leaving.

The fat man, who was among them, handed Raivine the rat he'd saved for her on his way out. "Enjoy it," he snarled.

CHAPTER 14

Raivine waited until all six were gone before passing the rat off to a child and dropping into the ventilation shaft, herself. She watched the last of Axle's crew follow a bend to the west.

She had told them they'd find Brian if they headed east. By going in the opposite direction, they had done exactly what she expected them to.

Axle would know she'd never give up Brian's location. With as much as she defended the stranger, he would expect her to send them the wrong way.

Which is exactly why she didn't.

But that didn't mean she had time to waste. They'd figure out soon enough that she'd outsmarted them and turn around.

Without a light of her own, Raivine scurried back toward the first underground exit from the ventilation shaft. She'd made the trip often enough to have it memorized. Pressing one hand to the wall on her left every few steps to keep her bearings, she walked quickly.

She was able to identify her destination by fingering

the cold, rough edges of the opening, but saw no indication of life. With one hand still on the cement, she whispered Brian's name.

The penlight came on.

She followed the beam into the tunnel. She took Brian's hand and said, "You in danger. Come."

"What's going on?"

"Father, angry. You go safe."

~

The tunnel took them to another ventilation shaft and from there Raivine led Brian another five hundred feet to a vent. Standing underneath it, she hit a button on the wall. The vent swung open. Then they climbed up the iron ladder that had been anchored to the wall and exited into an alley. Like the one by the club, the vent closed behind them on its own.

Two brick buildings left little room between them for pedestrians and kept most of the moonlight from reaching the ground. Still barefoot, he had yet to feel any dead bugs on the cement beneath his feet. Nor were there any large bins of bodies here.

Most likely the corpses were what brought the bugs, he speculated.

He had only a second to make the connection before Raivine was telling him to find the hidden pocket in his coat. She opened the left side of her own coat to reveal the lining and ripped open a previously sewn tear. She removed a chip the size of her thumbnail, pushed a tiny button, and palmed it in her right hand. "You do this," she said. "Protect against Palace."

Brian checked his jacket for the same stitched tear, activated an identical chip. He wasn't sure how the chip would protect him, but thought it best to do as she instructed.

Afterward, she peeled off a small piece of tape, also from inside her jacket, and taped the chip to the back of her hand.

Brian likewise checked inside his jacket for a piece of tape.

"No," she said. "You do this." She curled her hand into a fist to mimic holding the chip. Then she motioned for him to follow her.

The alley dumped them onto a crowded street. Dirty pedestrians shuffled by. Streetlamps flickered. Battered cars whined and coughed. It could have been one of the streets he'd been on before. Some things, like an electronics store with barred windows, he thought he recognized, but most things he didn't. Either way, it was all becoming alarmingly familiar.

When the *hell* was he going to wake up?

They weaved through the crowds, ducked into alleys, cut through parking lots to avoid the Enforcers. "Bad news," she called them, the first time they ducked out of sight. "Work . . ." She trailed off. At a loss for words, she pointed beyond the side street they were hiding on, across the main drag, and up.

At first, he could barely see the building rising into the night sky. Slowly, his eyes were able to discern the faint blue light shimmering on the glass walls, the unique architecture that · reminded him of an upside-down pyramid. Even though they were some distance away, he could tell the building must be as big as a skyscraper.

It was quite a contrast to the bland, small buildings everywhere else, but he wasn't surprised that he'd missed it before. He hadn't spent much time looking up at the sky.

The farther they went, the more Brian felt they were being watched. He shook off the idea as imagination, but asked anyway: "Are you sure being up here is safe? Aren't there tunnels we can take to get where we're going?"

"No tunnels," she answered.

Suddenly, Brian saw a stranger glance quickly, maybe too quickly, at them before his face was lost to the crowd. Nonsense, he reminded himself.

They made their last turn onto a roped off street at the edge of the city. Raivine picked up the pace until the darkness had swallowed them and the noise from the traffic was faint. Even this far away, though, she did not turn on her penlight. The moon provided enough visibility.

Along both sides of the street were houses, vaguely similar to those he might expect to see in his own world. With the moon above casting an eerie blue glow onto the roofs and no lights on behind their cracked windows or boarded up doors, they unnerved Brian the way the houses of a ghost town in the Old West might. Each seemed to ooze violence and unrest.

Occasionally they saw vagrants passed out or huddled around bottles of booze. None of them moved in any way threatening, though.

"Where are we?" Brian said.

"Home."

Before Brian could ask what she meant, he was distracted by the steel grate now underneath them. He knew immediately that it connected to the ventilation, though it didn't feel cold. "Hey. I thought you said there were no tunnels where we were going."

She looked down, struggled for words to explain a new concept. "Tunnels dead." She made a rumbling sound with her mouth while at the same time she violently shook her hands.

That could mean one of two things, Brian decided. They'd been brought down by an earthquake or poor craftsmanship. He'd have believed either one.

~

Raivine led him through the side door of a small brick house. The lock had already been broken. No wood panels barred their entrance.

This house, like all the others in the area, had been built as part of an expansion program funded by Leon's father during the territory's heyday. With artificial plants and trees imported to create the feeling of being in the countryside, the residential neighborhoods were popular with people looking to escape congested city living.

They sold fast.

However, years later, when the turbines that powered Drekar began to fail, Leon had no choice but to condemn these neighborhoods and shut off the pipelines that funneled electricity to them. There simply wasn't enough money in the city budget to keep all the turbines operational, his Financial Captain explained in the eviction notices that were sent out. Apologizing for the inconvenience and thanking residents for their sacrifices, the letters further advised the home owners that they had sixty days to evacuate and regrettably could not be compensated for their losses. The letter concluded with Leon Chricton's tired mantra: Never fear. Prosperous times lie ahead.

~

Inside, Brian found what he wouldn't have expected to find anywhere in this world, especially not in an abandoned house. Here he found a home. With a couch, rugs, and books. With vases of wilted flowers. With pictures hanging on walls. With floors, though dusty, clean enough to suggest they were at one time kept spotless.

Somebody had loved this house dearly.

Raivine turned on her penlight.

Brian walked over to the fireplace. He glanced across the photos on the mantel as Raivine moved to a hallway, then into a room. Immediately, he realized these pictures meant she hadn't picked this house at random.

"Home," she said when she returned. She dried her hair with a towel, and handed the towel to Brian. He did the same.

They looked at the pictures together. Some were of Raivine as a baby. Others were of her father. A woman, which Brian assumed was her mother, was in many of them. Dressed in clean clothes, they smiled with a happiness he hadn't seen since he'd arrived in this world.

He pointed to a picture of her mother. "What happened to her?"

A sad look washed over Raivine's face. Instead of answering, she said, "Come." She led him to the couch and then turned off the penlight to save batteries. Brian sat down, draped the towel over the back of the couch, and moved to place the chip he'd been carrying on the wooden table in front of them.

She stopped him, closing his fingers back around it. "Hold."

Then he heard from outside a thump-thump-thumping that sounded like a helicopter passing distantly overhead. Raivine, suddenly wide-eyed with fear, repeated her warning.

When the helicopter was gone, she released his hand

and asked, "Where you home?"

~

Like her father, she'd been wondering where he had come from. Had she been more comfortable with his language, she would have asked back in her quarters. But now, feeling strangely vulnerable surrounded by her past, she felt like she had the right to know. Even if she wouldn't understand every word he told her.

"Where am I from?" Brian repeated.

"You answer," she said, unaware of how rude it sounded. Had she understood the connotation, she would have said: *Please tell me. I'd really like to know.*

"I don't know where I'm from."

This time she was confused by the message instead of the words.

"I mean, I don't know where I'm from in this world, anyway. If I'm supposed to be from anywhere. In my world, I was born in Atlanta, Georgia. The USA. It's, um . . ." He trailed off, as if he believed she wouldn't understand.

But she got the gist of it. He wasn't from her world. He was from . . . someplace else.

Probably the same place as the robed one, said her father's voice in her head.

~

The tunnel led to more tunnels. Axle split his team at the first fork. With Noor and Sherri behind him, he ducked through the narrowest of the rocky passages.

Soon afterward, he came along a small crew digging a new branch to the north. They worked with pickaxes and shovels, wore coats to keep out the cold. "Have you seen Raivine come through this way?"

"Haven't seen the little darling," said one man. Another shook her head. Axle swore and doubled back.

Either the intruder had been hidden down the other passageway, in which case the other half of Axle's team would find him, or Raivine had outsmarted him.

~

The pale moonlight seeped through the living room windows.

Raivine, sitting with her back to those windows, looked as mysterious as a lost shadow. "I understand why Father worry," she said, though Brian couldn't see her lips move. "He good man. He confused."

Then, after a moment of silence, Brian asked, "Do you have any more pictures?"

"Pictures?"

"Pictures. Photos." He pointed in the direction of the mantel, though he could barely see where he was pointing. "Maybe an album?"

"Album?"

"A collection of pictures," he explained, waving his finger toward the mantel.

She understood. "Yes," she said. The tone in her voice revealed nothing. He couldn't tell how eager she was to share them. But she stood, crossed the room, and removed a thick leather-bound book from a shelf.

Once back on the couch, she opened the book and turned on her penlight.

Inside the book, he saw an assortment of pictures that suggested a happy childhood. In one, a young Raivine of seven or eight, grinning, probably laughing, stood in the front yard with her arms outstretched, ready to catch a ball of some sort. In another, she stood on her father's feet, her hands in his for stability as, Brian assumed, he danced her around the living room. A third was focused only on a medium-sized dog with long, silvery-white hair. All were labeled with characters he couldn't read.

"What do these say?" he asked, pointing to the text scribbled below the one with the dog.

Her eyes rolled up in thought. She pointed to the animal. "What you call?"

Brian told her.

She slid her fingers along the foreign characters and said, "'Dog: *Batin*.'" She skipped a character she couldn't translate. "'Six month. Raivine say favorite birthday present. She three years.'"

"What happened to him?"

140

"Run nowhere."

Ran away, Brian interpreted. That had to be disappointing. But instead of dwelling on it, maybe specifically not to dwell on it, stories of her childhood began to dribble out. As she struggled through Brian's language, she sounded as if she were telling them not only to him for the first time, but to herself as well.

In a way, perhaps because she genuinely had to concentrate on both the memories and the language, she was.

When she encountered a word she didn't know, she made hand gestures or pointed to objects in the photos to illustrate the idea. Once Brian told her the word she was looking for, she repeated it, and never had to ask again.

In a conversation reminiscent of charades, Brian learned that she had lived in this house since birth, and that she had been born at sunrise. Such a birth, when there was light on the streets but the heat had yet to sink its tentacles into the ground, was believed to be a sign of future fortune for the child.

And for the first seven years of her life, she said, she had indeed seemed blessed. Back then, her father was not the man she knew now. He was patient, kind, and trusting.

With her mother, they would take walks in the park or play board games or gather in the living room—this very room—to share the events of the day.

"I sit there," Raivine said, her shadowy hand moving toward a corner too dark to see.

That's how things used to be. Everyone had a job. The streets were clean. Children used to play in the park. There was no such thing as a cemetery, but the dead were not discarded; they were mourned, incinerated, their ashes kept.

Raivine glanced down to see Brain's pale, bare feet in the soft glow from outside.

Everyone had shoes.

But even back then the city had been quietly falling apart as war took its toll on the territory.

For Raivine's family, the extent of the problems had not been felt until her mother had fallen victim to a skin fungus, which first appeared as brownish-red spots on her right shoulder. Despite the use of ointments, her skin began to crack and itch. The fungus spread. In a second diagnosis, it was identified as something Raivine called *mordutulin*, a rare, but treatable, disease—had the right medicine been available.

Unfortunately, although the war had started strong, with Moriba's border towns nearly obliterated in the first wave of attacks years before, Moriba had rallied quickly. They sent troops to the frontline and leveraged their relationship with Orig to put a stop to any trade between Artubal and the other territories.

To his own citizens, once again broadcast from the massive Palace walls, Leon claimed this act of aggression demonstrated, without a doubt, Moriba's interest in destroying them. Then, in almost the same breath, he assured them they need not worry. He could still bring supplies in from overseas. "No one will starve. You have my word. Never fear. Prosperous times lie ahead."

What he didn't tell them, though, was that certain items, like medicines for rare diseases specific to the territories, would be impossible to obtain once supplies ran out. Or that jobs like Axle's, chief attendant at the main library, would soon be cut.

Due to the former, Sweeney, Raivine's mom, was not the only one suffering, Dr. Shirgarmo said.

Although Axle pleaded with him, begged him to find a way to get the medicine she needed, Shirgarmo, who was then saner and sober, was reluctant to make any promises.

But you will try.

Hmmmm, I will try.

Then Axle took Raivine and Sweeney home where they did the only thing they could do—wait. Except for Axle's weekly and then daily calls to Shirgarmo, they tried to pretend that everything was fine.

Still, Raivine could remember how her mother had changed after that day. Her laughter wasn't as deep, her smiles were somber, her eyes always seemed just on the edge of tears.

At night, Axle would rub various creams into the infected skin to relieve some of the discomfort. He would tell her everything would be all right. Shirgarmo would come through. He had to.

Sweeney and Raivine, who was barely ten at this time,

both knew Axle was mistaken. There was nothing the doctor could do. But neither one said so, because they both also knew Axle needed to believe that Shirgarmo might fulfill his promise.

Within three months the infection had spread down her back, onto both arms, and was inching toward her stomach.

It hurt to move.

She spent most days in bed, practically soaking in lotion. Axle had started phoning Shirgarmo two to three times a day. When the doctor told him that it no longer mattered whether he could get the medicine, the infection had spread too much, the phone calls stopped. Axle, head down, quietly walked out the back door, slid down the side of the house, and cried.

For hours, he cried.

Raivine never told him that she'd been watching him sob through the kitchen window. Axle was a proud man. He wouldn't want his family to see him in pain. Especially his daughter. Raivine knew that he thought of himself as her hero, and he was right. So she let him keep his dignity. As much as she wanted to run to him, hug him, cry with him, she didn't. She buried her tears.

After she'd seen all she could stand, she went upstairs where she sat on the edge of her mother's bed and played cards until Axle returned.

Sweeny died in her sleep. Another year passed with her ashes in an urn on Axle's bedside table. Meanwhile,

Raivine began fifth grade in a building badly needing repairs. And then . . .

She stopped talking. She glanced awkwardly at the chip taped to the back of her hand and sighed.

CHAPTER 15

She wanted to tell him how The Resistance came to be.

She wanted to tell him that shortly after her mother died, The Palace had condemned the suburban neighborhood where she had grown up, forcing Axle and her to move into a small one-bedroom apartment in the city. Although the suburban neighborhoods were the first to suffer from the failing turbines, The Palace soon announced that there would be scheduled rolling blackouts across the city to further conserve power.

As if Axle had been personally targeted, the library at which he'd worked was permanently closed the same week.

In the only apartment he could afford, Axle slept on a couch that had its cushions worn to the springs and gave Riavine full use of the bedroom. Besides the couch, the furnishings provided by the owner included a foldout metal table, two plastic chairs, and a bed that sagged in the middle. The walls had been painted white years ago, but now that paint had yellowed in large spots and chipped away along the edge of the ceiling.

With them, they had brought only a few things from their former lives, partly because the apartment was small and also because The Palace had assured the suburban families they would be able to return to their houses once the war was over and the turbines could be fixed. Although Axle didn't believe that would be any time soon, he didn't want his eleven-year-old daughter any more worried than she already was.

And it was the many mementoes and furnishings that they had left behind which made this house feel like a home.

Still grieving the loss of his wife, angry about the loss of his home, sad to be raising his daughter in a small and dirty apartment, and worried about his dwindling savings and the lack of job prospects, Axle reached out to the men and women with whom he had protested years before. Like Axle, they had opposed the Honesty Chip, disapproved of Leon's rule. Most of them still did.

For three months following, while Raivine was at school, he held weekly meetings in his apartment with other likeminded citizens. They discussed Leon and the decline of the territory. They collectively agreed that Moriba was not behind the rail line or the war. They discussed new protest plans. They considered a march and a sit-in. But secretly, in the darkest recesses of their minds, they knew a peaceful response would be ignored. Just like their protests against the Honesty Chip.

Still—united not by profession, organization, or ideology, but by their hatred for Leon Chricton and his leadership—they wanted to do something.

They weren't the only ones.

While they numbered barely a dozen in the first meeting, they didn't stay that small for long. Members told friends and friends became members.

When the group outgrew the apartment, they moved their meetings to an abandoned warehouse titled to a small-business owner; with his shop now closed, he had no need for the space. And as the numbers grew, it wasn't just the location that changed. The conversation changed, too.

Protest wouldn't be enough, Axle finally said. They had to do more.

The conversation shifted to revolution.

After a series of intense sessions, during which tempers soared and disagreements nearly led to fights on more than one occasion, the forty-four men and women finally seemed to reach a consensus. Their territory had traveled too far down the path of self-destruction to be saved from within. If they wanted to turn the tide, they needed more than new leadership—they needed Moriba. But, unlike Leon's vision, Axle believed that to claim it through war was not the way to merge the territories. By the time such a victory was won, Moriba might be nothing but devastated factories and blighted farmland.

Rather, the way to merge the territories was for them to surrender themselves to Moriba's rule. Moriba's laws were fair. The territory was prosperous. If the citizens of the two could work harmoniously, lives on both sides of the border could be improved. Where the citizens from Artubal would benefit from Moriba's existing production and farming infrastructure, Moriba, which struggled to meet the production demands for popular exports, could benefit from the additional labor force and real estate.

Unfortunately, whispered conversations of the group and their meetings eased through the city on the wings of gossip until they reached an off-duty Enforcer. From there, the news was quickly fired up the chain of command until it got to Leon Chricton. Unrest he could understand. Protests he could tolerate. But talk of revolution must be extinguished.

Immediately, he sent an Enforcer, dressed in street clothes, to watch the building for another meeting. When people started to arrive the next night, Leon dispatched more.

These Enforcers were sent uniformed and armed. Their orders were to arrest or kill everyone in the warehouse.

The only blessing of the attack, albeit small, Axle would tell Raivine later, was that most members of the group had not yet arrived. Only five were there when the Enforcers charged in, guns pulled, shouting for the group to surrender.

One man tried to run and was immediately shot in the back. The other four were hauled away.

Axle knew all this because he'd watched it happen.

He had been only two blocks away when the caravan of Enforcers soared past him. Immediately he stopped, ducked behind the corner of a building, and watched. As the drama unfolded, two more members of the group approached Axle from behind. "Go back. Warn the others," he told them. "Get whatever you need from your homes—blankets, pillows, clothes, any food that won't spoil, anything you can carry—and get to the library. You're not going to be safe at your homes after tonight."

He knew at least one of the four arrested would break quickly, giving up the names of everyone else.

Then he fished around in his pocket for his key chain, removed a single key. He handed it to one of the men. "This will get you into the library." When their eyes asked why he still had the key, he shrugged. "They never asked for it back. Now, go!"

And as they headed in one direction, he took off in another.

He went straight to Dr. Shirgarmo. By this time, the doctor had already started drinking during the day. He did so to chase away the demons, he said. Too many people were dying. Too many who could be saved if only the territories around Artubal weren't blocking the import of needed medicines. However, he was not yet the half-crazed lush he would become over the next decade.

With nothing to lose, Axle told him about the group and begged for his help. "We're going underground," he

150

said to the doctor. "We have no choice."

"What can I do?" Dr. Shirgarmo asked, without hesitation.

"I need you to take out my chip. Mine and those in the other members of my group."

"That's dangerous."

"We don't have any choice."

"I've never done it before."

"I know. Nobody has."

"You know what will happen if I make a mistake. . . ."

The Palace had claimed that the removal of the chip would only be attempted by somebody interested in committing crimes much more severe. For that reason, removing the chip was punishable by death. No second chances. The Palace also announced that the punishment would be administered by the chip, itself. But nobody knew how.

"Don't make a mistake."

The doctor nodded nervously. "OK."

When all the men and women of Axle's group had gathered in the basement of the library, as well as their children and any extended families they had nearby, Axle introduced everyone to his daughter and the doctor.

The room was lighted by a fire that burned in a steel tin. Bookshelves filled with dusty books extended deep into the darkness beyond, organized into rows, labeled by subject.

Around Axle, the families were spread out in a semicircle. Worry formed lines in their foreheads and presented as tremors in their hands.

"Listen to me, everyone," he said. "We are here now not because we are traitors, as The Palace would no doubt like you to think. We are here because we believe in a better world for ourselves, for our children. We are here because we are willing to stand up for that belief. While things are dark now, they will not be dark forever. Trust me, support each other, and be patient. We will fight. We will win. We are the resistance!"

A roar of support rose up from the crowd and the name stuck. From that day forward, they were *The Resistance*.

Once the crowd quieted, one woman asked, "But where will we live?"

"Here," Axle answered, extending his arms outward, as if he were presenting a vast and desirable plot of land.

"In this basement?"

"Not just. Directly below that grate runs a ventilation shaft." He pointed to a corner hidden by the murky blackness surrounding the small band of rebels. The vent had been added because of the maintenance workers' complaints—the long distances they had to travel underground through the chilly air to reach the heart of the cooling system. Because of the serpentine nature of the tunnels, none of the original vents was less than half a mile from the machinery. The library, on the other hand, was almost right on top of it. "From this haven, we have access to hundreds of miles of tunnels which will connect us to almost every point in the city. We'll be able to access other abandoned buildings. And where the ventilation doesn't go, we'll make tunnels of our own.

"Before we get started on that, though, we need to address a more pressing matter." He paused, allowing the crowd a moment to prepare themselves for the reason he'd introduced them to Dr. Shirgarmo. Then, when he felt they were ready, he said, "We need to remove our Honesty Chips."

Immediately, the members of The Resistance began to murmur in hushed, anxious tones.

"I know it's dangerous. But the alternative is worse. It won't be long before The Palace knows our names. Once they do, they'll start tracking us. If they catch us, we'll be sent to the Artubal Cells, and if what we've all heard about that place is true, then you know as well as I do it's worse than death."

More murmurs.

"Now, to show you how much faith I have in Dr. Shirgarmo—"

Before he could finish the announcement, a heavyset, burly man with beady, blue eyes and a large chin stepped forward. "I'll do it," he said.

His name was Dox. Axle didn't know his last name. He only knew the man had formerly worked at one of the shipyards along the coast. Dox considered himself "tougher than stone." He wasn't afraid of anything, he'd said more than once. "I'm sure not afraid of a little surgery," he said, when Axle asked him if he understood the risks.

"Are you certain?" Axle asked.

"If it weren't for you, we wouldn't have any chance, at all. Besides, if he's as good as you seem to think, I've got nothing to worry about."

However, it was a confidence that would cost him his life.

During the procedure, Dox was fully conscious and lying on the ground. His eyes were open, his jaw clenched.

Dr. Shirgarmo cut into his hand. Since he did not yet understand how the poison was released, he took several moments to study the chip through the telephoto lens attached to one side of a pair of glasses. He noted the tiny clamps that extended from each side of the chip and wrapped around tendons, holding it in place. Then, near the wrist, he observed a needle that resembled a beak. His best guess, which would turn out to be correct, was that the poison would be ejected from this beak.

But there was no way to tell what would trigger it.

He decided to proceed cautiously. He would cut one leg at a time until he could gently lift the chip out of Dox's hand.

When he made the first cut, though, the needle extended and punctured a hole in the vein underneath it. The doctor froze, horrified. He saw no poison discolor the blood stream. For a brief moment, he assumed none had been released.

Then, a few seconds later, Dox began convulsing, foaming at the mouth. His eyes rolled back.

The doctor pushed him onto his side to keep him from choking on the foam. "I . . . I . . . " He was unable to find words. He didn't know what else to do.

Dox shook violently for fifteen seconds before he stopped and was still.

Nobody spoke.

Dr. Shirgarmo checked his pulse, then shook his head solemnly in Axle's direction. The volunteer was dead. The doctor closed Dox's eyelids.

As Axle looked across the room at worried faces, he knew what everyone was thinking: *Will that happen to me?*

Immediately, he kneeled beside the doctor and asked him what went wrong.

"It's the tamper response The Palace warned us about. When I cut the first clamp, the chip reacted."

Around Axle and the doctor, the silence had broken. The members of The Resistance began to panic.

"Do you know how to prevent it next time?"

"I think so."

"How sure are you?"

The doctor nodded, licked his lips. "I'm sure."

Axle once again addressed the crowd: "People, please, calm down. I realize this is a tragic moment. It's tragic for all of us. I can only take comfort, as all of you should, that he leaves behind no family to mourn him. He died a hero. His sacrifice brought to light invaluable knowledge about the behavior of the Honesty Chip. Without his contribution, we would all be dead. And Dr. Shirgarmo has just assured me that he now knows how to perform the procedure safely."

A shout from the back of the room: "What if he's wrong again?"

"What choice do we have?" Axle responded. "Go back to the surface, if you want. Wait for the Enforcers to come take you away." He scanned his eyes across the crowd, daring anyone to leave. When no one did, he lay on the ground and stretched out his right arm, palm down. "Take out the chip, doctor."

"Father!" Raivine screamed. She was so young, so scared. She ran to him.

Axle pushed himself up to his knees. He grabbed his daughter by her arms.

She was wearing a long gray dress that hung loose on her body. As tears streamed down her cheeks, she said, "Don't do it, Father. Don't." Her gaze drifted to the dead man, who was only feet away.

Axle shook her to direct her attention back to him. "Hey, it'll be fine. I promise."

"You won't be fine. Father, please don't."

"Have I ever lied to you?"

She shook her head no.

"Do you think I'm lying to you now?"

A little slower this time, she again shook her head no.

"Trust me, I will never leave you. Nothing bad is going to happen to me." He gave her a long hug, then kissed her forehead. He wiped away her tears with his thumbs. "I love you. Now, go stand over there," he said pointing in the general direction of the crowd.

An old woman, dressed in a white shirt and ill-fitting pants, walked up behind Raivine and placed her hands on the girl's shoulders. Axle didn't recognize her. Probably, like the children, she had been brought down here to protect her from The Palace. Nobody knew to what lengths they would go to find traitors. But nobody believed they were above torturing an old woman or a child to learn their location. "Come on," she said to Raivine. "Your father will be all right."

Reluctantly, Raivine allowed herself to be led away from her father. During the procedure, she kept her eyes closed, hands over them, face pressed against the leg of the woman. She didn't look in his direction again until she heard applause.

"That, my friends, is why Dr. Shirgarmo is here."

Trading the darkness behind her hands for the fire-lighted basement, she saw her father standing, right arm raised so everyone could see the stitched scar on the back of his hand. Blood trickled from it.

"Now, who's next?" he said. "We need to do this quickly."

A young man raised his hand. "I'll go next," he said,

nervously.

"Very good! Very good! Come on over here. You needn't worry about a thing. It'll be fine."

And it was.

Dr. Shirgarmo removed the chips one by one. As there was no anesthesia available, many patients cried or screamed during the procedure, but nobody else died.

When the surgeries were complete, Axle, with the help of several men, pushed the bookshelves back to the walls, stacking them two, three deep, to make as much livable room as possible. Others pried off the grate. From there, the rebels explored and mapped the underground ventilation shafts. They assigned responsibilities to each member of the group. They organized the children by age for the purposes of continuing their education.

Axle, using the information he'd found in the library's chemistry books, built homemade explosives to collapse the roof. Considering the rampant decay of buildings across the territory, nobody would suspect the collapse to be anything more than the inevitable failure of the building's supports. Not only was he right in his assumption, but The Palace used the collapse as justification for closing the library months earlier. It was irrefutable proof that the building had been unsafe. Had The Palace not shut it down, who knows how many lives might have been lost?

Inspired by the successful collapse, The Resistance leaned on Axle repeatedly to provide the small explosives tunnel workers needed to blow holes in and out of the ventilation shafts as they extended their underground network.

Meanwhile, Dr. Shirgarmo found new recruits and sympathizers who were willing to donate food, clothing, and other goods.

Slowly, The Resistance grew.

CHAPTER 16

Raivine wanted to tell Brian all of this, but she was exhausted from the lengthy and challenging stories she had already told. Besides, with her limited vocabulary, she wasn't sure how much the story about her mom he'd understood or how much he would understand if she went into the history of The Resistance.

~

"My mother died, too," Brian said, hoping to put her at ease, hoping that their shared pain might keep her talking. Although he hadn't understood everything Raivine had tried to convey, he'd caught the highlights. The stories lent him a better understanding of his environment, but, more importantly, he understood how sharing her memories helped her deal with them.

She didn't keep talking, though. Instead, she lowered her head, eyes on the floor, as if the past had momentarily overtaken her.

Then she said, perhaps to change the subject, "How

your words look?"

If she didn't want to talk about her past any further, he wouldn't push. He asked for a pencil.

Once she understood what he wanted, Raivine left the room. She returned with a feather, an ink well, and a piece of paper.

Brian asked her to read the text below one of the photos.

"Ball. Run. Father."

After dipping the sharp end of the feather in ink, he put together the words for her. When he was done, she read what he'd written several times. Then she asked, "How spell 'Brian'?"

He wrote it down for her.

"Raivine?"

He wrote that, too, adding the *I*s and switching the *N* and *E* to account for the unusual pronunciation. With her name on the paper, he looked at her, and added below it: "A beautiful lost angel."

She smiled sweetly. "Lost angel" was not in her vocabulary. She studied the page some more. "Huh."

Then came an uneasy feeling in his stomach as he remembered that the girl in the hospital had used that phrase "lost angel." However, he quickly rationalized it by reminding himself that this was a dream. Just a dream. Vivid. Detailed. Drug inspired. But how could it be anything else? How could it?

~

Raivine knew better than to spend much time at the house. She had to get back underground. She had to find out the truth behind the robbery if she were ever to convince Axle that he could trust Brian.

She stood, folded the piece of paper Brian had given her, and shoved it into her coat pocket. "I must go."

"But—"

"I return soon. Promise." Quickly and awkwardly, she kissed his cheek, thanked him as well as she could for yanking her out of the way of the falling stalactite, and fled into the kitchen like a ghost.

Brian followed, imagining how vulnerable he would feel if left alone in this strange, dark house in this strange, dark world. "You can't go."

"I come soon," she said, without slowing her pace.

"Well . . . can you at least leave me the flashlight?"

She hesitated at the door, glanced back at him. She removed three thick candles—red, white, and green—and a box of matches from a drawer. The candles were wide enough at the base to stand upright without assistance. She lit the red one, partially hollowed out from previous use. "Use one, one, one. I return before darkness." She squeezed his right hand. "Never lose chip." Then she left before he could say another word.

~

Loneliness crept in. He heard the hollow echo of a breeze he could have sworn wasn't there before. A nearby cabinet seemed to dance in the flickering candlelight.

Helplessness knotted in his chest, suffocating the momentary high he had felt when Raivine had kissed him.

He didn't understand this world, what had happened to it, or what was happening to him. Had he believed it was real, he would have sworn that the devil, himself, had claimed it as his own.

CHAPTER 17

Rock made the jump with no greater ease than Brian had on his first visit. Since neither Maine nor Lester had asked Brian about the physical challenges of the transition, he couldn't have anticipated the vomiting. Although he'd seen Brian's clothes fall to the floor when the boy had been force-fed the pill, he hadn't expected to be without his own. However, what had alarmed him most was that he found himself unarmed. The dangers lurking in this unknown world could be infinite.

Alone in a warehouse, he walked to the nearest window and looked down at the busy street below. Quickly, he put his thoughts together. Brian was out there somewhere. But before he could start searching for him, he'd have to find clothes and a weapon.

And he'd have to work fast.

Despite Steven's assurances that he would eventually return on his own, Rock worried that the secret to making the return trip might be something only Brian had figured out.

But the risk was worth half-a-million bucks to Maine,

who had grown impatient waiting for Brian to return—and that had been enough money for Rock's greed to cloud his judgment.

In search of an exit, the ex-boxer was feeling his way along the wall when he tripped over a body hidden by the shadows. The homeless man flopped to his side and moaned, but didn't wake up.

Rock hesitated, frozen, hand balled into a fist, ready to strike if the man moved again.

Once he realized the homeless man wasn't getting up, he leaned over to smell his breath. The stench of alcohol was unmistakable. The homeless man was passed out drunk.

Rock wasted no time stripping him of his clothes. The pants were a perfect fit—a small piece of luck, since the scuffed leather shoes cramped his toes and the right sole had come partially unstitched.

Now wearing a rough, wool tee shirt, he found the exit, descended a flight of rickety metal stairs, and made a right onto a moderately busy road.

Choppers thumped through the distant sky, none close enough to cause worry.

He stopped a man to ask where he could find a pawn shop, or a gun shop, and the man replied in a language he couldn't understand.

"Foreigners," Rock said, with disgust.

After stopping several more people, he realized that nobody spoke English.

He was a stranger to everything here. *He* was the foreigner. That meant he would have to be extremely careful. If this world were anything like his own, he knew that the wrong gesture, even unintentional, could anger an otherwise rational person. The wrong action could send some to draw arms.

No, he told himself, he'd have to be more than careful. He'd have to be self-sufficient. Keep a low profile. Find a weapon, find Brian, and go home.

He wandered from one street to another and browsed small, grimy shops that looked promising, only to find himself still unarmed more than two hours later. Instinctively, he avoided the men in the shiny, black uniforms as he assumed they were officers of the law and might not take kindly to an outsider. He couldn't have imagined that they could identify him as a stranger before a word was ever spoken simply by scanning him for an Honesty Chip. One might last days or even weeks undetected if he was lucky, but nobody without the chip would go undiscovered forever.

~

Four days passed. Smelly, dirty, and weak from living on discarded food, Rock was losing hope of ever finding Brian, of ever returning to his world.

What he didn't know was that when he had shifted dimensions, he had also shifted back through time. As far as he knew, time moved in only one direction, at only one speed.

Years in the future, the scientific community would be shaken to its core by the discovery that the relationship between time and space, specifically the space between dimensions, was unstable. Point A on one timeline did not always align with its corresponding point on another timeline, and shifting between the two could actually send you slightly forward or backward through either one.

When Brian finally crossed Rock's path, he was with a woman. She was nobody he recognized. But then, he hardly recognized Brian.

He'd been shuffling along a busy street when they moved past him in the other direction.

As hope bloomed, he turned to follow. He kept a safe distance, hid himself in the crowd, and fell even farther back when the crowd started to thin. He trailed them to a roped-off street and fell back again. Then, he went to a house, where he parked himself around a corner and watched the door.

He could have barged in, but decided he didn't like the odds. Since he'd arrived in this world, he'd found no better weapon than a butter knife he stole from a second-hand shop. The woman, likely a native, could be carrying something more substantial. Besides, Brian was the one he was after. There was no reason to get her involved.

So he waited.

He remained crouched until his legs became sore.

When they did, he put one knee down on the dusty artificial grass beneath him. In his hand, he held the knife tightly by its handle, ready to use it if anyone snuck up on him.

If Brian and the woman left together, he'd follow them farther. If they parted ways here, Brian would be his.

His other knee and one hand hit the ground to take more weight off his tired legs. He'd been without sleep since he arrived. His body felt drained.

Overhead he heard a chopper again. This one came close enough for him to see it. It didn't look like he had expected it to. If pressed for a description, he would have said it looked like a giant, robotic fly, with the thump-thump-thumping coming not from blades but from matching wings. It hovered high in the air and from below its crystal green eyes came a ray of yellow light.

The ray encompassed him. As much as he wanted to run, his body refused to move. Frozen by fear, he tried to imagine what might happen next. Nothing did. Almost as soon as the chopper spotted him, it banked right and flew away.

Very strange, he thought.

The woman left, but he waited a full minute after the shadows had enveloped her before quietly entering the house through the back door.

He inched through the kitchen toward the flickering candlelight in the living room and found his mark sitting alone on the couch with a photo album open on his lap.

Brian turned a page, didn't look up.

~

As soon as Rock stepped onto the wooden floor in the living room, the house creaked. Brian's head immediately twisted up and around. His eyes caught Rock's. Seeing one of the men who had kidnapped him from the hotel, Brian realized that not even here, in an empty house in a dream, would he get any peace from his nightmare. There was always somebody coming for him. "Why can't you just leave me alone?!?"

With the knife tucked into the sleeve of his shirt, Rock said, "Relax. It's time to go home."

Brian put the photo album on the table and stood. He kept the chip Raivine had given him tightly clamped in his right hand.

It's just a dream.

He looked down. His fist was balled so tight that his fingers had turned white. He loosened his grip; color returned.

Rock was about to say something else when suddenly they heard a helicopter thumping toward them. The sound grew loud enough for Brian to realize that there must be more than one. Then, small beams of yellow light penetrated the windows from above.

Rock glanced up at the ceiling, and produced the knife. "Dammit, Dore, we have to go home now!" He shouted as much to be heard as to be threatening, as much from his fear of the choppers as his fear that he'd be stuck in this world without Brian's help.

Suddenly, the men in shiny, black uniforms kicked in the front door as others came through the rear. The flashlights mounted on top of their guns scanned the interior. They shouted things neither Rock nor Brian could understand.

One grabbed Rock by the back of his throat. In an attempt to defend himself, he spun around, his knife out, as if the blade might be able to tear through his attacker's armor. The officer, as Rock called him, clutched a hand around his wrist, squeezing until tendons throbbed, muscles involuntarily contracted, and the knife fell.

Unless they shot him, Brian still had a couple of feet to maneuver, and a couple of seconds. For reasons unknown, all of their attention seemed to be on Rock. Still, he'd seen too much lately to believe he would remain unharmed if he waited around.

Brian retreated to the nearest armchair. With all his might, he slung it at the large bay window. The glass shattered into a thousand small slivers that glistened in the light and fell to the floor like rain.

In all the commotion, he also dropped the chip, though he didn't know it until he felt it crush underneath his bare foot. Suddenly, all the officers jerked their heads toward him with new interest.

He still didn't understand how the chip worked. But,

in that moment, he realized that it had somehow made him invincible to these armed men.

What had actually happened was not so mystical. The chip he had been holding was identical in function, although not design, to those most citizens still had implanted. It, like all the others, regularly sent out a weak signal detectable to Enforcers in the immediate vicinity. Aiming a small handheld device that resembled an electric razor at any citizen nearby, an Enforcer could immediately tell if his target had a chip implanted based on the subsequent audio alert he received from the small ear bud inserted in his left ear. An alert was also triggered if a chip suddenly stopped broadcasting within an Enforcer's vicinity. Unlike the former alert, which was a simple beep or buzz, depending on the outcome of the scan, the one that signaled a broken broadcast was a whiny, crackling hee-haw, like the sound of an aging police siren from the fifties, unmistakable no matter how noisy the environment.

It was this signal that had drawn their attention when Brian stepped on the chip.

But he had no time to figure any of that out right now.

He dived through the window and rolled over the broken glass. The thinnest pieces lodged into his back and arms. Others sliced through his pants, into his legs.

Pain coursed through his body, more real than the headache he'd felt earlier, more real than the hunger which had once again started to stir.

Back on his feet, he ran. Down the darkened street,

away from its roped-off entrance, away from the boxy, black cars that had brought the officers.

He heard the *whump-whump-whump* of blades slicing wind and looked up to see four bug-like choppers surrounding the house. Another two were following him. They weaved back and forth, their bright yellow spotlights shining on the ground. A single beam honed in on him, so he veered off the street, out of its sight.

He ran across the artificial turf and past the artificial plants that made the neighborhood feel so suburban.

It didn't take his pursuers long to catch up. He heard the footsteps of officers gaining ground behind him and rammed open the door of a nearby house.

While he couldn't see the choppers anymore, he could hear them circling. *Christ!* Maybe they'd leave.

Then, the officers busted through the door.

He ran from one room to the next, looking for another way out. The dim light from outside revealed shadowy furniture, furniture he dodged as he maneuvered through a kitchen, living room, dining room, den. Most of the doors were boarded on the outside, which meant they could still open inward. He found one that led off to the side, threw the lock, and slid underneath the boards that barred entrance.

To his right, he saw more officers approaching, shouting. He though one of them was repeatedly saying: "You . . ."

You stop. Maybe.

He turned the other way, kept running.

More officers appeared from between the two houses ahead of him. They seemed to have doubled in number. He turned right at the next alley, just feet from being caught. But the officers kept up, and the choppers kept their spotlights on him.

Before he had a chance to choose which turn to make next, an officer tackled him, and stuck him in the arm with a needle. He fell into a haze.

CHAPTER 18

The drug wasn't enough to knock him unconscious, but it left his brain swimming, making resistance impossible. Two officers hoisted him back to his feet and led him to one of the black cars. With their mission complete, the choppers overhead faded into the distant sky.

Now unable to feel the glass poking his flesh, he was placed into the backseat next to Rock. "Hey," he said, with everything he saw curling and twisting in on itself.

Rock chuckled, smirking from the same drug.

Two officers climbed into the front seats, and the fleet sped back into the city—past the drunks, past the rope at the street's end—hurrying to reach their destination.

"Why are . . . why . . . ," Brian began, then lost himself in the scenery that whizzed past. Pedestrians and buildings contorted into strange shapes outside Rock's window.

"Why what?" Rock asked. His face had turned a bright red. His grin was as wide as a Cheshire cat's. If anyone he knew had seen him now, they wouldn't have known he was the same man.

Suddenly, Brian slapped Rock's knee. They both laughed. He no longer felt threatened by the ex-boxer. A cool, comforting numbness seeped through his body, making him giddy. If anything, he was ready to call Rock his friend. "Why are you here?"

"What do you mean?"

"Nobody else is in my dream." He looked at the officers and laughed again. "I mean, nobody else that's real is in my dream."

∼

Rock's eyes glazed over. In his current state, he couldn't immediately grasp Brian's limited understanding of the world around him. He answered with a question of his own: "How do we get home?"

"I wake up, silly. Ah, what am I telling you that for? You're just in my head, right? So you already know that."

Slowly, understanding sunk in. Brian, Rock's best hope for shifting back, thought this world wasn't real. That only made him laugh more. "I'm not in your head."

"No?"

Shaking his head fervently, Rock said, "Nooooo."

∼

They came to a sudden halt. The driver rolled down his window. Before them stood a large steel wall—maybe fifteen feet high and polished to a shine.

The driver reached his right hand over his body, out the window. He shoved it, palm down, into an oval-shaped hole on one side of an upright steel tube. A bright blue light blinked on and off inside the opening.

Looking out his own window, Brian said, "That's cool."

"What? What's he doing?"

Something to do with the chip. . . . But Brian couldn't hold onto his thought long enough to finish it.

Then the wall seemed to part at an invisible seam, sliding into itself, revealing a long cement road in the car's headlights.

They started moving again. Beyond the wall, the desert seemed to stretch out infinitely from either side of the car. Scattered fires dotted the landscape, around which men and women huddled for warmth. "If you're not in my head, why are you here?" Brian finally asked.

"If all this isn't real, why did you run?"

"Even in dreams, you run when you're scared. Especially in the ones that seem real." He considered the statement particularly insightful, until he forgot what he said.

"That's true," Rock agreed. He looked through the grill that divided the front and back seats, and saw the upside-down pyramid towering before them. Bright lights around it shined from out of the sand, trickling up its cloudy, glass walls. "What's that?"

176

The driver shouted something over his shoulder as he banged the grill with his fist.

Rock slumped back into his seat.

"The Palace," Brian answered.

"It's huge."

"Yeah."

Something large and mechanical skulked in front of The Palace.

"What's that?" Rock asked.

Brian tried to focus on the swirling, metallic creature. "Don't know."

"You knew about The Palace."

"The what?" They both laughed again.

"The Palace."

"Yeah, I knew about The Palace."

"So, what's that?"

Brian watched the metallic creature cross in front of the lights. It moved on long legs, was maybe two stories tall. It reminded Brian of . . . but then it was gone, enveloped by the darkness. "Don't know."

As they closed in on The Palace, they could see that it didn't stand on the very tip of a pyramid as it appeared to from a distance, but its base was not much wider than a point—too narrow, in fact, to support the giant structure on top of it. Yet, it stood.

The road took them through a door in that narrow base and they parked in an open steel bay. The other four cars parked behind them.

Every surface here was as polished as the steel wall that surrounded The Palace. Fluorescent lights were mounted to high ceilings. An elevated walkway ran along three of the bay walls. A passage, wide enough for a car or small truck, stood open underneath that walkway. Other doors were only wide enough for foot traffic.

Four of the officers escorted Brian and Rock up a flight of stairs to the walkway and through one of the smaller doors while men in brown jumpsuits drove the vehicles through the opening under the platform.

"Hey, how can I get me one of these Palace-type things?" Rock asked, smirking. He stumbled on wobbly legs and an officer grabbed his arm to keep him from falling.

Brian knew he should be afraid, he knew he shouldn't willingly accompany these men to whatever destination they had in mind. But he wasn't afraid. The drug dancing in his brain wouldn't let him feel fear. His thoughts were too scattered to consider escape, or even to remember that he should.

White hallways with unmarked doors running along both walls led to an elevator with a glass ceiling and white tile floor, up three flights, into more hallways. They passed other officers in their shiny uniforms and staff in white jumpsuits performing indiscernible jobs. They entered another steel room, much smaller than the bay. Here, six steel tables were lined up in pairs. Each had dozens of small holes scattered across the top with steel clamps for wrists and ankles. To Brian, they looked a little like one of the tables in Maine's sub-level lab.

"Those don't look friendly," he said.

His droll understatement made Rock laugh.

Neither resisted as the officers led them to the center pair of tables and locked them down.

"Compromising position you have us in," Rock joked. But the officers only responded by leaving the room, flipping off the light.

~

Hours passed. The drug wore off. The pain from the shards of glass embedded in Brian's skin returned. The fear that he couldn't grab hold of before caught up to him. Despite the cool air, sweat beaded on his face and under his arms. He moaned as a subtle shift at his torso sunk a piece of glass deeper into his body.

Although Rock still lay on the table next to him, he didn't say a word.

Despite the playfulness the drug had produced, Rock was not his friend. Besides, it was—

I'm not in your head.

—all—

No?

—just a—

Nooooo.

Suddenly, Rock shouted: "Get me out of here, you

179

bastards! If you don't, I will crush your skulls!" Rock, who, as a boy, had been beaten down until he was bloody on the Seattle streets, whose job had put him face to face with violent criminals on more than a dozen occasions, was terrified. Then the big bulldog of a man whispered to Brian, "Please, tell me how we get back to our timeline."

Before Brian could say anything, or even decide what to say, the door opened.

Two men entered. One was dressed in a pressed black suit with buttons that ran from waist to neck; he was scruffy, with wild black hair and even wilder gray eyes. He looked worn down by fatigue. The lines on his face had been hardened by unspeakable cruelty.

The man behind him was draped in a long blue robe that covered his hands and most of his face.

"Let me out of here, you pieces of shit!" Rock screamed.

They ignored him. The man in black asked a question and the man in the robe pointed at Brian. In English, he said, "Him."

"You better set me free or I will eat you for dinner!"

The wild-eyed man walked over to a panel on the wall, opened it. Inside were a series of buttons and levers.

Brian watched, but didn't say a word. He worried again about the risk of dying in a dream.

"What are you doing? Let me go!"

The man pressed a button.

"Now!"

A motor groaned.

"Dammit, I said—"

He pressed a lever up, pushed another button. Rock couldn't finish his last sentence before spikes, three feet long, shot up through the holes in the table. They ripped through flesh, split bone, came out the top of his body dripping with blood. Rock buckled, screamed. Seconds later, his head flopped to the side and he fell silent. Brian could see in his empty eyes a lingering pain. Was he dead yet? For Rock's sake, Brian hoped so.

"Don't worry," the man in the robe said to Brian. "This will not happen to you." As he spoke, the wild-eyed beast behind him moved away from the wall panel.

"Why did it have to happen to him?"

"Because he's not you."

"I don't understand. What's going on?"

The man in the robe took two steps toward Brian's feet so that Brian wouldn't have to strain his neck as much to see him. "Trust me when I say you understand less than you think you do."

Brian squeezed his eyes shut. *I want to wake up right now. Right now. . . .*

"Right now," the man in the robe said. Brian opened his eyes, feeling like his most private thoughts had been violated. When the man in the robe spoke again, Brian's fears were confirmed. "You want to wake up right now." The man in the robe smirked briefly underneath his hood. "You will soon. Very soon. That's not important *right*

181

now.

"What is important is that you understand what's going on. Leon Chricton, the gentleman standing by your head, rules this territory. Between you and me, he is one sick son of a bitch." Another smirk.

Brian was surprised to hear such a familiar phrase come out of the stranger's mouth. Shawn used to say that a lot, didn't he? Then, he wasn't surprised anymore, because, so help everything holy, this *was* a dream.

"And, in my opinion, he's more than just a little insane."

Brian glanced at Leon, expecting him to lash out at the man in the robe for speaking ill of him.

"Don't worry. He can't understand me. He thinks I'm telling you about something else, which I will, in a minute. First I need to make sure you realize that his problems, the way he chooses to run his territory, are not your problem. His problems with The Resistance—Axle and Raivine— are not your problems. They think they're fighting the good fight, but they're going to lose. That's what I want to make sure you understand. If you come back here again, they'll drag you down with them."

"I won't come back."

After all, it's all just a stupid dream!

"Think hard before you do. The only reason you're alive is because I've made certain promises to The Palace. They know that if anyone tries to hurt you I will see to their demise. I know, you're wondering what promises,

182

and why I should care that you're alive. Don't dwell on it." Suddenly, the man in the robe disappeared from one side of the table and reappeared on the other. "Hopefully you'll never have to find out.

"Now to the matter at hand. . . . I've explained to Leon that you will be leaving soon and *won't* be coming back. When that happens, well, let's just say it keeps the future less complicated. I told him there was no reason to go forward with the surgery or the imprisonment, but he insists." The man in the robe sighed and took a step backward. He said something to Leon.

"What surgery?"

"It won't be as bad as you think."

Without further explanation, the man in the robe followed Leon out of the room, turning off the light as he left. More hours passed. The hunger that had flirted with Brian before began to consume him. He felt as if his stomach had turned on his other organs, eating him from the inside out. He worried about the surgery. He worried about waking up. His mouth went dry. His skin crawled when he thought about the rotting corpse to his right— would a malfunction send spikes up through him before someone returned?

~

When the lights came on again, a small group of people entered rolling a gurney. They were dressed in knee-length, gray smocks. Two men. Two women. The women had their hair pulled back into ponytails. All four wore rubber caps and rubber gloves.

Two officers followed behind them. They released the clamps around Brain's ankles first, grabbed hold of his feet to make sure he couldn't kick anyone. Afterward, they removed the clamps around his wrists.

They slung him, kicking and bucking, onto the gurney. Strapped him down. Wheeled him through more hallways.

The next room he saw housed a surgical chair of some sort and medical supplies. But his thoughts were running too fast to focus on anything. He wanted to—*had* to—get out of here.

When am I going to wake up?

Soon. The man in the robe had said so.

They freed one hand to turn it over.

How the hell would he know when I am going to wake up?

Then they strapped the hand back down. A woman with a shaved head entered from a door along the wall adjacent to the gurney and slipped on white gloves. Leon and the robed man followed her in. At the same time, one of the men who had brought him here removed a small plastic container from a cabinet. He opened it, revealing some sort of computer chip.

"*Lartata, nor dosd*," said the woman with the shaved head to someone beyond Brian's field of vision. Then she used a scalpel to make an incision in the back of his hand.

He screamed from the pain. The man with the plastic container handed the surgeon a chip, which she placed under his skin.

Somewhere beneath his racing thoughts—*Wake up now, Brian! Wake up now!*—he realized what was going on, why Raivine had taken an interest in his hand at the club, underground; why she'd given him a similar chip to carry as they navigated the city, why she told him never to let go of it, why the officers had only been interested in Rock until Brian had accidently crushed the chip underfoot. Everyone under Leon's rule had one. Somehow they marked you, made you traceable.

Suddenly, tiny metallic clamps shot out from the sides of the chip and knotted themselves into the flesh of Brian's hand. The pain was worse than that of the surgeon's cut.

Brian screamed. The surgeon shouted something else. Somebody gave her a needle and thread. She daftly sewed his skin back together. Each prick of the needle seemed to hurt worse than the one before it. Just when the pain was at its most intense—just when Brian felt like he was about to pass out, couldn't scream any louder, just when the surgeon cut the thread, ending the operation—everything went black. A sickness took hold of his gut. He faded to nothing.

CHAPTER 19

The robed man, known as The Mystic in Drekar, followed Leon Chricton out of the room. Leon turned to speak, probably to insist that The Mystic not forget his promise. But before he could, The Mystic said, "If you'll excuse me, I have personal business to handle."

Without another word, The Mystic vanished from the hallway and appeared in the desert outside The Palace doors. One of the large robotic guards, which looked and moved like a spider, rotated toward him quick enough to suggest alarm. Then he vanished again, appearing in the surrounding city, just on the other side of the tall steel walls.

For personal reasons, he had hoped Brian would not be captured. Now he could only pray that Brian would not return. No matter how much he might still try to help the outsider, he knew that if Brian shifted one more time into his world, forces would be put into motion that would be hard to stop. Almost impossible. And if they weren't stopped, Brian would never be the same man again. Never again. . . .

Never again. . . .

He shook off the thought, vanished, and materialized inside a ventilation shaft below the city.

Through the grate above street lamps flickered. The metal clanged underneath heavy foot traffic.

Although it was not yet obvious to The Resistance, The Mystic knew Noor was responsible for Brian's capture.

He would not get away with that.

The Mystic shifted one last time.

~

Along with seven other members of The Resistance, Noor slept in a natural cavern with low ceilings, no plant life, and no stalactites or stalagmites. For tonight, he'd claimed a corner, far from the fire and the others who shared the space. It had taken him several weeks to adjust to sleeping on the ground, but he was used to it now.

His mangy, brown coat was draped over him like a blanket.

In Noor's dream, the day came back to him in disjointed flashes.

"He's involved!" Axle had bellowed. He was shouting at Raivine. They had found her in the ventilation shafts while searching for Brian.

"Karta! Can't you hear yourself, Father? You're being single-minded. The only thing you know is that

somebody *gassed the guards. Wouldn't it make more sense if the people responsible were already in our midst? Or at least spoke our language?"* She looked at Noor, Sherri, a hairy man called Auver, and the others behind him. Her eyes pleaded for help. *"This is a witch hunt. Don't do this. You've let him alone so far and what harm has he caused?"*

With both Axle's and Raivine's flashlights on, the tunnel was brighter than usual. The swirling blue air looked especially rich, the gray walls almost white with frost.

"This isn't you, Father."

"We have to protect The Resistance," Noor said.

"He doesn't even have a chip," Sherri added.

"We can't let all of our work come crumbling down for one man," said a skinny fellow from the back of the group.

"He was probably born inside The Palace walls," added another. "Raised there. I bet that's why he doesn't have a chip."

"Do you hear yourselves?" Raivine said. "Father, please. This is going too far."

"Helping The Palace steal our artillery was going too far!"

"Father, don't get caught up in this madness. Let's do a proper investigation before we jump to conclusions."

"I don't have time for this," Axle said. "Where is he?"

Raivine looked away and said in a whisper:

"Somewhere safe."

A moment passed. The only movement was the subtle shift of light pushing at shadows. To Noor, it felt like three, four, five seconds, but he wasn't sure. Don't back down, he silently pleaded with Axle.

Then, Axle stormed past his daughter. "I know where he is!"

"What?" Noor shouted, darting forward to keep pace.

Axle stopped to face his team. "We can't all go. Together we'll attract too much attention. Noor, you come with me."

"I'm coming, too," Raivine said.

"Don't you think you've done enough damage for one day—conspiring with the enemy? I swear you're lucky you're my daughter and I know you well enough to know that this is just a horrible mistake on your part."

"Axle!"

"Fine. If you want to come, come. Don't think you're going to stop me from doing what's right, though." He looked at the others. "The rest of you go back."

The dream skipped ahead, past their ascension into the city, down the streets, to the house.

Axle slowed his stride as he neared his old home. "I haven't been here in a long time," he said, barely loud enough for anybody to here.

"Not since I was very young," Raivine added.

A few more steps, and they saw the shattered bay window. "What do you think happened here?" Noor asked.

Raivine walked to the window. Staring at the ground, she shook her head. "They took him." She sounded heartbroken.

In the glow of her penlight, she saw the bloody shards of glass on the ground, the bloody footprints that ran onto the street. "He tried to run. . . ." She pressed her thumb and first finger to her eyes to hold back tears. She took a deep breath. "He couldn't have gotten very far."

"This could mean anything," Noor insisted.

"What else could it mean!?"

"Anything." The word slipped meekly out of his mouth. Utterly powerless.

"Do you see now, Father? Do you see? Look what your suspicion has done. This wouldn't have happened if you had trusted him . . . or me, even." She took a deep breath. "He was an innocent man." She rubbed her eyes again. "We have to do something."

Axle looked down at the aftermath by his feet, ashamed of his misguided suspicion. Noor knew what he was thinking: He had been so sure Brian was to blame, because Noor seemed so sure. Could they both have been wrong?

Then Axle said the only thing he could, because it was the only think he knew to be true. "There's nothing we can do right now."

~

"Wake up," whispered a voice, and Noor did. His eyes shot open with alarm. A hand covering his mouth kept him from screaming. Staring hard into the shadows, he recognized the man crouching over him as The Mystic. "Meet me in the tunnels. We have to talk."

The Mystic vanished.

Noor pushed himself up onto the palms of his hands. The fire had nearly gone out. Everyone else in the room was asleep. He slipped on his coat and scampered out a hole in the floor.

When he dropped into the rocky tunnel beneath the cavern, he immediately turned on his penlight, and almost screamed when he saw The Mystic less than a foot away. At just under six feet, The Mystic towered over Noor. Although intimidated, he said, "You're taking a huge risk coming down here, you know."

"This is important."

"What is it about?"

The Mystic gestured toward the south tunnel. "Let's walk."

"Sure." But he didn't move.

"You in front."

Noor knew something wasn't right. The Mystic was *never* supposed to come down here. He tried to swallow his fear. "Why?"

"You have the flashlight."

~

They walked in silence for a long time, ducking underneath roots that hung from the ceiling, dodging rocks that protruded from the walls at odd angles. Eventually they moved from the tunnels made of rock and earth to those of the ventilation system. "What did you want to tell me?" Noor asked.

"I know what you've done."

Noor stopped and turned around. "Excuse me?"

"Keep walking."

Without any argument, Noor did. He knew better than to defy The Mystic's commands. That is, if the stories were true . . . if even half of the stories were true.

"I thought you'd be smarter this time."

"I don't understand."

"I want you to make this right. . . . OK, now stop."

Noor looked up. He was standing immediately underneath the library. He could barely remember being guided through the right forks to get here. He could barely believe this was their destination. "What do you want me to do?"

The Mystic answered only by raising a hand. As if in response to his command, the cold, blue air that was funneled through the shaft began to swirl around Noor. Suddenly, The Mystic flicked his wrist upward, lifting Noor off his feet and sending him through the rectangular opening above.

He landed on top of a sleeping woman who groaned as he rolled off. She sat up. Then The Mystic was beside him again. "Call for Axle. Wake everyone up."

"You're crazy. Why are you doing this?"

The woman on the floor stared at The Mystic in wonder and in fear.

Noor felt something in the pit of his stomach begin to twist and burn. Pain welled up. He knew it was The Mystic's handiwork. He shouted Axle's name with all his might, as if hollering for his savior.

The pain in his stomach subsided.

Of her own volition, and out of fear alone, the woman screamed too. She crawled over comrades to get as far away from the robed one as she could. Children awoke, groped for their mothers. Not even the toughest men among The Resistance dared to do more than retreat.

~

"What's going on?" Axle shouted when he opened the door to his quarters. He hadn't yet assembled the scene in his mind and couldn't understand what had stricken everyone with such terror.

"Tell him!"

Axle's gaze shot across the fire to The Mystic. As his own heart fluttered, he understood the panic.

"Tell him who's responsible," The Mystic said.

"If I do that . . ." The painful knotting in Noor's gut

193

returned. "I am!" he shouted, right after Raivine stepped through the doorway behind Axle.

"Tell everyone to stop screaming," The Mystic instructed Noor.

"Stop screaming! Everyone, please! Stop!" Noor shouted until he had everyone's attention.

"Now tell them what you've done."

"I thought we were on the same side," Noor whispered. He didn't understand what he had done wrong. Playing on Axle's natural suspicion, he had convinced Axle that Brian must be working with The Palace. But so what? Why should The Mystic care? Framing Brian was the best way to conceal his own actions.

"I can make this much worse for you."

Not daring to waste a second with The Mystic's threat looming over him, he spent no more time trying to figure out why The Mystic wanted him to confess. "Axle, I'm sorry!" He started to tremble. "I lied to you. I manipulated you. I convinced you that Brian was involved in the weapons theft. I convinced you that he had come to spy on us. He hadn't."

The crowd whispered to each other with surprise.

Axle, now understanding that he wasn't in danger, took a step forward. "It was you?"

"It was me! It was . . ." He turned to The Mystic. "Please don't make me do this." But the only answer The Mystic gave was to manipulate the air again, to sweep him off his feet and drop him hard onto his knees. Pain shot from his kneecaps up through his hips. "It was me!"

"Show him the proof," The Mystic said.

Noor removed two small glass canisters from his pocket. He held them out, palm up. A clear liquid was visibly bobbing in each one. "See?"

Everyone knew what they were and how they worked. When the glass broke, *Lyzarda* inside mixed with oxygen, to form a deadly, colorless gas.

"These are what I used to kill the guards."

The Mystic swiped the capsules out of Noor's hand. He summoned Sherri over.

She approached with caution, accepted the capsules, and, following The Mystic's instructions, delivered them to Axle.

Axle looked at them, pocketed them. "If the Enforcers thought we had no more weapons, why didn't they attack us after the theft?"

"Because nobody was supposed to kill Brian," Noor said. He finally understood why The Mystic had blown Noor's cover. It wasn't just the Enforcers who were not supposed to kill Brian—*nobody* was supposed to kill Brian. And what might Axle do but that if he truly thought the outsider an enemy? "They knew that if they came in shooting Brian might get killed."

"Why would they care?"

"Because he's an outsider," Noor said, his words coming out in one long whine. There were so many other ways he could have concealed his actions, he realized. It was now so obvious that he shouldn't have framed Brian after The Palace had promised to protect the outsider. He had been foolish, and his regret over his naivety brought him to tears. "He's special," he finally continued. "That's what they tell me. I swear that's all I know about him. I don't even know if they understand why he's special."

~

Axle's face drew long. Everything Noor was saying had to be true. It made sense. Brian's unexpected arrival had saved them, not hurt them.

"You understand who the traitor is now?" The Mystic asked Axle.

He nodded. "I do," he said gravely.

"Then I'll leave Noor with you. Do with him as you see fit." And with that, The Mystic disappeared.

CHAPTER 20

Brian didn't have time to roll to his knees before he vomited. Stomach acid only, this time. That strange, leafy plant, which he still didn't believe he'd eaten, had been digested many hours before.

But he had made it to his side, and the vomit drained down his cheek instead of lodging itself in his windpipe.

With his eyes still closed, he ran one hand along the carpet underneath him. Carpet—that was a good sign. (His hotel room had carpet; unfortunately, so had Maine's lab.) But it didn't necessarily mean he was awake. What if this turned out to be a new dream, or a more horrific part of his last?

Realizing all of these were options, he lay where he was for a while, too scared to open his eyes. He was exhausted, weak. He desperately wanted the dream to be over; he needed the dream to be over.

There's no place like home, he mouthed. *There's no place like home.*

Please let this be the hotel room. Just a dream. Just a dream.

As he continued to run his left hand across the soft carpet, its fibers tickled his palm. And he stayed like that, hopeful that he was awake, feeling an unexplainable pity for the people who inhabited his dream world—

There's no place like home.

—until the burn in his throat became unbearable and the numbness that stretched along his back gave way to the pain of a thousand tiny cuts.

He squeezed his eyes tighter until a single tear rolled down his cheek. Now he could feel the cuts on his feet, too.

He wasn't awake.

When he finally moved, it was only because he needed a cup of water to wash down the burn in his throat. He pushed himself up. He reminded himself that nothing behind his closed eyelids was real. Finally, he opened them.

At first, he could barely believe what he saw. Even in the darkened room, shadows cast by the green and yellow lights of computers told him where he was—

I'm back in the lab.

Then new worries set in. Where were the boxers he'd been wearing? Where were the men who had kidnapped him? Where was Mr. Maine?

The cuts . . .

How had he gotten the cuts?

Something wasn't right.

He found a light switch by the door and flipped it on.

Walking on his shredded feet hurt less than he would have expected. He searched for broken bottles or beakers, but found none. How had he cut himself?

When he saw the recent surgery to his right hand, he began to panic. His heart rate picked up. As if triggered by recognition, the wound began to throb.

He tried to think. He tried to remember. He tried to piece everything together. The answers were right there, right there . . .

This didn't seem like a dream. None of it had seemed like a dream. But the rest had been too strange to be real.

Then he remembered Rock pleading with him.

Please, tell me how we get back to our timeline.

Begging: *Please get us home.*

You're just in my head, he had told Rock.

I'm not in your head.

Then more voices.

Shawn Ryder: *Jerry, you know, one of the janitors, thinks it might be like LSD, only way more intense.*

But it wasn't LSD. Having experienced the world twice, Brian could say that much for sure.

Kerri White: *Sounds like science fiction to me, boys.*

Maybe it wasn't science fiction, either.

Tell me how we get back to our timeline.

Finally, Rock's words sunk in.

It was real.

There wasn't a better explanation. The surgery to his hand was certainly real. So were the cuts on his body.

Although Steven Lester could have done both of those things while Brian was unconscious, he knew that the scientist hadn't.

Furthermore, why would Maine have asked him all those questions if it had only been a dream?

The idea was overwhelming, and left Brain short of breath. Suddenly lightheaded, he leaned against the wall so he wouldn't fall over.

Tell me how we get back to our timeline.

~

Nobody had moved since The Mystic vanished. Except for the crackling fire and a young girl sniffling to hold back her tears, the library was silent and still. Noor glanced from the hole, his only exit, to the eyes watching him. In those eyes, he could see only one emotion—hatred.

Axle approached. "How could you?" he asked, stepping through the crowd.

"I don't know," Noor answered, his voice quivering. As he spoke, his gaze darted to and from the hole. He could run, he thought; he still had a lead. But then he figured he'd never make it to the surface. As quick as he was, there were others in the library who were quicker.

"How could you?!?" Axle shouted.

"When The Resistance started, I believed in it. I believed in it as much as anybody. But it's been so long.

So many years have passed and where are we? Living underground like animals, that's where."

"I nearly . . . Well, I don't know what I would have done to Brian if we had found him tonight."

Noor said nothing.

"I trusted you." Axle was at arm's length, his face flushed with anger. He called for Mikel Sar and Nicktar Arart to escort the traitor into his quarters. Having done physical labor all their lives, they were both big, rugged. Either one of them could have handled Noor on his own.

Mikel's most identifiable characteristic was that he had one blue eye and one green eye, an unusual genetic abnormality. Nicktar's was his crooked nose, broken repeatedly in back-alley fights for cash.

The two men grabbed Noor's arms, just below his shoulders, and dragged him into Axle's quarters. They shoved him inside.

He stumbled forward, fell to his knees.

"Thank you," Axle said to them as they left, closing the door behind them.

"I should kill you!" Axle shouted at Noor, once they were alone.

Staying on his knees, cowering, hand up to protect his face in case Axle swung at him, Noor whimpered, "Please . . ."

Infuriated, Axle kicked him in the stomach. Noor doubled over, groaning.

"Artubal is nearing its end and all you're doing is

making it that much harder for the territory to recover," Noor spat. "At least Leon Chricton is trying to do something to help."

"You mean by blaming Moriba for our downfall even though they're not responsible? By starting a war with them, isolating us from the other territories? If Leon cared about the people more than his power, he'd have turned over the territory to Moriba a long time ago."

"They would have let us die."

"They have no interest in letting us die."

"Leon told me he tried to hammer out a treaty with them and they refused."

"You believe him?"

"At least he's doing something! The weapons Moriba sends—they're just manipulating us to help them take over!" Noor shouted, still on his knees.

Axle kicked him in the stomach again, knocking the wind out of him.

Noor fell to his side this time and curled into the fetal position.

"What else did you tell him?" Axle demanded.

"What else is there to tell? That we hide out underground, sleeping on dirt?"

Axle dropped to one knee. He grabbed Noor by the shirt with his left hand and pulled him so close their noses almost touched. He balled his right hand into a fist. The candlelight illuminating the room flickered in his eyes, intensifying the hatred and betrayal Noor saw in them.

"This will get worse," he whispered. Then he let go of Noor's shirt and punched him across the jaw.

Noor rolled onto his back. Blood dripped down his cheek from a split lip.

"You've helped them. Now you're going to help us."

"Why should I?" Noor asked, his voice cracking. Although he sounded defeated, beaten, and afraid, he seemed to have found the courage he had lacked when standing next to The Mystic.

Up until now, Axle had been asked to name those within The Resistance least likely to betray him, Noor would have made the top of the list, second only to his daughter. Noor had protested with him against the Honesty Chip. Like Axle, he'd suffered the loss of both his job and his home due to Palace cutbacks. For him to betray The Resistance and defend The Palace with such passion, he must indeed believe The Resistance was incapable of saving Artubal. This thought was disheartening for Axle. He worried that there might be others within The Resistance who had the same doubts.

He had to restore confidence within his followers. He could no longer wait until Moriba delivered word that they'd sufficiently weakened Leon's frontline forces.

And the information Noor had in his head about The Palace might be exactly what he needed to do that. He would do whatever it took to get that information out. No one man was more important than the mission.

He called Mikel and Nicktar back into his chambers

and told them to bring a rope. While neither made Axle's inner-circle of confidants, they were nearby and perfect for a job that relied on brute force alone.

"What are you doing?" Noor asked.

"Tie him up," Axle said, when the men entered, ignoring Noor's question.

The rope was long enough to reach from one pillar to another and back.

The two men grabbed Noor's hands and feet.

"What are you doing?" Noor asked again, shouting this time, his voice wounded by desperation.

"You'll tell me what I want to know," Axle answered.

Coughing, spitting blood, Noor tried to resist the two men who now had hold of him, but the effort was futile. Soon, Noor's feet were bound by the rope attached to one pillar, his wrists by the rope attached to another. In between, he lay on the ground, stretched out and vulnerable.

"Thank you," Axle said to the men. This time, though, he asked them to stay. And they did, hovering over Noor, their faces twisted with disgust.

"You've been inside The Palace," Axle said. Then, looking down on Noor from the side opposite Mikel and Nicktar, he slammed the heel of his boot into his stomach.

~

Every muscle in Noor's body tightened up. His

stomach burned. His side ached. With tears again forming, he thought the last kick may have cracked a rib.

On some days since he'd met with Leon, he'd regretted his decision to betray The Resistance. But then he reminded himself of the things Leon had told him, which restored his confidence that his new loyalty was well placed.

Although he'd been a coward much of his life, he did not want to die as one. He would keep the things he'd learned about The Palace to himself . . . or so he planned, until Axle pulled his knife from his boot and shoved the blade underneath the fingernail of Noor's left pinky.

Axle twisted the blade, prying the nail out of its bed.

Unimaginable, white-hot pain shot up his arm from the tip of his finger. As he hollered and cried, he heard Axle say, "Nine more to go. Then we start on the toes. After that, I'll cut off your ear."

~

"All right! All right, I'll tell you!" Noor screamed. "Whatever you want to know, ask me. Just, please, stop."

"You've been inside The Palace?"

"Yes," he said, through fresh tears.

"How do we get inside?"

"You can't."

Axle held his knife up so Noor could see it. There was still blood on the tip. "Nail number two coming off."

"OK, stop. An armored truck brings provisions from the coast to The Palace every sixteen hours. Usually it's just carrying food. It came in while I was there so I know it's true."

"How many men?"

"Just two, I think."

Axle kicked him in the ribs again.

Noor screamed. Through shallow breaths, gritted teeth, he said, "I really can't be sure. I think it's just two."

Axle sighed, but didn't push the issue further. Noor could only know what he'd seen. He moved on. "What kind of security is at the gate?"

"You'll need a chip to get inside. It'll need to be one that's got permission to let you through. I don't know how to get one of those."

"Let us worry about that. What else?"

"That's it. Nothing else until you get inside."

"Don't lie to me."

"I'm not! I swear!"

"When we get inside, what floor are Leon Chricton's chambers on?"

"Seventeen. Top floor."

"Do you know when the next delivery is?"

"Every sixteen hours, like I said. That's what Leon told me. Ten o'clock."

"What makes you so sure?"

"That's what time it was last time I was there." Since the people of Artubal counted their hours to sixteen instead of twenty-four, the time had been easy to remember.

Axle tapped the blade of the knife against his cheek.

"Are you going to let me go?" Noor asked. "Please, let me go."

Axle cut the ropes.

"Thank you," Noor repeated several times, slithering out of the knots.

As he did, Axle pulled a history book off a shelf. He ripped out the tattered, blank pages from the back. Next, he removed a sharpened stick and an inkwell from a small, wooden box in the corner. He put everything down in front of Noor. "Draw it for me."

Cowering on his knees, Noor asked, "What?"

"The Palace! Draw a map of The Palace!"

The candles flickered as the traitor went to work. He unscrewed the inkwell and dipped in the sharpened stick. His hands trembling, he started to map The Palace interior as quickly as he could.

"Go tell Raivine to get the team together," Axle said to Mikel.

~

Brian stood—frozen, naked, within feet of that horrific-looking monstrosity that might be an electric chair, and might be something far more sinister. He struggled with his expanded reality. He worried that Maine might return at any moment. He tried to understand how he fit into this complex puzzle.

Something had led him here.

Why?

Then he remembered the girl in the hospital. Raven. Hooked up to so many machines. Throat slashed.

Raivine!

He knew what he had to do. *Somehow* he had to save her. Because she was okay in her world. . . .

But in this world . . .

He squeezed his eyes shut as hard as he could, rubbed his temples.

Something . . .

Something . . .

Something that he couldn't quite get his mind around was still missing. She couldn't be in both worlds at once.

But she was.

Which could only mean that when she had shifted from one dimension to the other, she had also slid through time.

Maybe that's what had happened to Brian on his first trip. Maybe he had gone forward in time. That would explain why he'd lost a day.

While it seemed bizarre to him, it was the only thing that made any sense.

He had shifted not just through dimensions, but time as well.

He looked around the empty room. His boxers weren't on the floor. He was alone. Nobody was coming for him because nobody knew he was here.

He had shifted through time again.

Forward?

Backward?

It didn't matter just yet. The only thing that mattered was getting back over to the other world and saving Raivine.

While she had already been attacked in his world, she hadn't in hers. Perhaps if he could get back there, he could save her. In some small way, doing so might also make things right, might balance out his failure to protect Flanders.

Although she had warned him not to go, although the robed one had warned him not to return, he would have to try.

~

Including Raivine and himself, Axle's team consisted of two women and three men. Before Noor had finished his maps, they were all gathered in Axle's chambers.

They knew why they had been summoned. None of them could believe the time had finally come, though. For all these long years, The Resistance had never made a strike on The Palace. Noor put down the sharpened, ink-stained stick he had been using to write and said he was done. "That's all I can remember."

Axle scooped up the pages and reviewed them. The

sketches were small, not to scale, with large sections marked as UNKNOWN. Even with all its flaws, the information was invaluable.

He told the two men who had dragged Noor into his chambers to take him away. They did not need to be present for the conversation that would follow.

"Do with him whatever you want. Break his legs, I don't care. Just make sure he can't get to the surface."

"You promised me you'd let me live!" Noor shouted as the men dragged him out of the room.

"I did no such thing," Axle responded. Then he turned to his team: "We need a plan."

~

Brian used a pair of tweezers to pick the remaining glass out of his feet. As he pulled the shards from his skin, he clenched his teeth. Sitting uneasily in the electric chair, he dropped them into a beaker he'd taken from the adjoining room.

Both the tweezers and the beaker he'd found with relative ease. It was almost as if he'd known exactly where to look, almost as if he'd been in the lab before. Of course, he hadn't. He hadn't even known it existed until he had been abducted from his hotel room.

When he was finished, he dumped the shards into the garbage and returned the tweezers and beaker to the very places from which he had taken them. Since he didn't know where he was in time, he wanted to leave as few clues behind as possible.

Also in the room where he'd found the beaker were two white lab coats. Hanging on a rack in the corner, they were long enough to cover him to the knees. Since he dared not walk the Atlanta streets naked, he took one. It buttoned in front and hid everything that mattered. Then he searched the shelves along the walls until he found a bottle of Diaxium. He'd need that to bring Raivine back to his world.

The rats squeaked from inside their cages. Steel balls in their water bottles bobbed up and down with small tick-tick-ticks. The air conditioning turned on and off with a groan. The computers beeped. Every sound played on his nerves.

He was desperate to get out before being discovered. If he could have left the glass in his feet, walked outside naked, or even left without the drug, he would have.

~

The pickaxe came down hard on Noor's right knee first, then his left. Kneecaps shattered. Flesh tore. His screams echoed down the rocky caverns, through the ventilation shafts and grates above, onto the city streets. Though after so much distance they had dissipated to little more than whispers.

He would never walk again.

Mikel used a rope to bind the traitor's hands and shoved a rag into his mouth.

Then Nicktar dumped him into a pit they'd discovered two months back. At twelve feet deep, it might as well have been a tomb for Noor. He would remain trapped there until he died.

~

No access code was necessary to leave the room, nor was a key necessary to summon the elevator from the sub-level. Maine figured that keeping people out was more important than keeping them in. Anybody Maine had wanted to keep in, he could chain up.

Between the lab and the elevator, Brian glanced up at the security camera. He remembered seeing himself on the monitor, in the lab coat, holding onto the bottle of pills.

Immediately he knew where he was in time. Maine had told him the robbery had happened Sunday night.

Once outside the Omega building, he tried to get his mind around this new impossibility. Maine's goons had kidnapped him because he had stolen something from Omega that he couldn't have stolen if he hadn't been kidnapped.

Yet something had made this impossibility possible.

Very soon he would find out what it was. For now, however, he chose to shake off this new puzzle piece and focus on how he was going to get the pills over to the other dimension.

People on the sidewalks stared at him. Cars stopped. With wide eyes, gaping jaws, and pointing fingers, they stared. He tried to ignore them.

Eventually, he ducked into an alley to escape their curiosity. Barefoot, like in the other world, he was thankful that he'd not yet stepped on any broken glass. He hunkered down against the wall. The shadows concealed him.

He was so tired. So very tired. It was hard to think. His hunger had worsened.

He folded his arms onto his knees and dropped his head. For ten minutes or more he wallowed in self-pity. He sniffled, shivered, and asked God: *Why me? Why me?*

Then he cried. For Flanders and his parents, for the children underground and for Raivine.

Any other day, any other time, he would have despised himself for playing the victim. But here, shrouded in the safety of darkness, comforted by the sounds of a city he knew well, his guard collapsed.

Slowly he found strength. He tapped into reserves he didn't know he had, reserves strengthened by the knowledge that if he gave up now—oh, how he would love to give up now—Raivine would suffer needlessly.

He put the bottle of pills into his left coat pocket, wiped away his tears, and gently pressed the tender flesh of his right hand with his thumb. Blood rushed toward the stitched scar and provided some relief from the throbbing.

There was a chip under there, he told himself, and wondered if it could broadcast between dimensions.

There's a chip under there.

He laughed, almost maniacally.

He finally had a plan. When he stole the pills from the lab, he knew he'd need to find a way to get them to the other world if he wanted to bring Raivine back, but he didn't know how he was going to do it. Now the solution was so obvious he could hardly believe it hadn't occurred to him sooner.

CHAPTER 21

Axle passed around the maps Noor had drawn, beginning with Sherri. The rest of his team consisted of Raivine, of course; Abot Zarst, the youngest of them all and classically handsome; and Auver Oparida, who hid behind a nappy beard and layered plaid shirts.

The five rebels sat in a circle in the center of the room.

"Are you certain about this?" Sherri asked, referring to the plan they had all agreed to.

"It's the best chance we'll ever get to take down Leon Chricton," Axle said.

Abot squeezed his sweaty palms together and nervously twiddled his thumbs. Strands of blond hair, long enough to touch his nose, fell haphazardly in front of his face, obstructing his view.

A candle in the corner burned to the quick and died. There was still plenty of light; nobody lit a new one.

"What if we don't make it back?" Abot asked.

"Better dead fighting than dead here," Auver grunted.

"They've been underground, Abot," Axle said. "They know where we are now. How long do you think it will be

215

until they return?"

Sherri looked at her watch. The band was worn, the glass cracked. The hour markers counted to sixteen. "Tonight's delivery will be coming soon," she said. If they wanted to strike tonight, they would have to act fast. "We need to make preparations."

Axle looked at Abot. "If you're not up to it, I don't want you coming with us."

"You need me."

"Can you handle it?"

Abot wiped his palms on his pants, pushed his hair away from his face. "It's like Auver said, I guess. We're going to die there or we're going to die here. I suppose we might not get another chance."

Axle nodded. "Go get ready."

Abot, Auver, and Sherri stood. They filed out of the room with Sherri in the rear. When she passed Axle, she hesitated. "I thought the robed one was working for The Palace. No matter how special Brian might be, why would he turn on one of his own the way he did Noor?"

"I don't know. I've heard about men with his talents living out in the land beyond the territories. I've heard that living there can make you insane. Maybe he doesn't even know why he turned on Noor."

"But—"

"Go get ready. It doesn't really matter right now, does it?"

Sherri walked away.

~

When Sherri returned, she was wearing a long, gray dress that was only inches from dragging on the ground. Underneath, she had a pillow taped to her stomach, creating the illusion of being pregnant. Her blond hair had been pulled into a bun. She had washed in an underground stream, so not a speck of dirt could be found on her anywhere.

Auver and Abot still wore the ratty, second-hand clothes that had been passed down to them by sympathizers. Weapons were the only provisions they required. These they had obtained from the few remaining in the training arena.

Once they had all returned, Auver gave guns to Raivine and Axle while Abot gave one to Sherri.

Sherri pulled up her dress. Without flinching, she ripped off the long piece of tape she had stuck to her leg. Then, placing the gun against her inner thigh, she used her free hand to wrap the tape around her leg and the weapon, securing it in place.

With final preparations made, Axle quickly led his team to a rusty, silver car parked on the surface behind an abandoned school building. It was sleek and small. Its frame, from nose to tail, was designed with a fluidity that almost made the car look as if it had been built from a single piece of steel. Its tires, twenty-two inches wide, extended far beyond the space intended by the wheel wells. A customized powerhouse of speed and stability, the car was a throwback to the glory days of the territory, a luxury vehicle when it first came off the assembly line and rarely seen today.

Auver, Abot, and Raivine squeezed into the back seat. Sherri took the front passenger seat. Axle turned on the one working headlight and sped from the parking lot.

The car bounced over the cracked roads as the headlight cut through the foggy night sky. They weaved around half-lighted brick buildings and dark storefronts with closed metal gates. They swerved around cars, narrowly missed the few surface dwellers who were still awake.

"Can't you be more careful?" Abot asked, gripping the back of Sherri's seat.

Sherri glanced at her watch. Since the decision had been made to strike tonight, too much time had passed. Anticipating the route the delivery truck would take, and accounting for the difference in time between the location where they would intercept it and The Palace gate, they were counting seconds. "Two minutes, seven seconds."

"If they're not early," Axle said. Suddenly, the rear of a large truck backed out of a parking garage in front of them. He slammed on the breaks. The tires screeched. Sherri put a hand on the dash to brace herself. Auver swore loudly with excitement.

Axle threw the car into reverse, then turned quickly off

the road onto a narrow one-way alley.

"We're going the wrong way!" shouted Abot.

A pair of headlights appeared from a side street, putting them on a collision course with another car. Its horn screamed.

Abot covered his head with his hands. Uselessly, he shouted, "Please, slow down!"

They were twenty feet from an accident before the building beside them gave way to another alley. Axle spun the car to the left.

"One minute."

Two more quick turns and Axle slammed on the brakes, skidded into an intersection. "This is it. Everyone out." He directed Auver and Abot across the road and told them to hide behind the side of the building. They did. He and Raivine ran back to the building behind him. This would be easy, he told himself as he pulled his gun from underneath his coat.

He watched as Sherri propped herself up against the car's rear tire. Her legs were stretched wide and cocked up at the knee. She put her hands on her stomach. Nervous beads of sweat dripped down her forehead.

Axle's hand tightened around the gun.

Then, they waited.

After almost ten minutes, the large, armored truck came into view.

From his hiding place, Axle saw the truck's headlights chase away the shadows around Sherri. He knew the

Enforcers were close, but without looking around the side of the building, he couldn't be sure how close.

Sherri slid down even more so that she was almost lying flat on the road. She shrieked as if in pain, began breathing like she was in labor. Tires squealed and Axle heard the clank of steel boots on cement as the driver climbed out of the truck.

"Move out of the road!"

Sherri wiped the sweat off her cheek. Her brown eyes sparkled in the headlights. "I can't." She arched her back as her knees shook and she shrieked again. "Please help me."

The Enforcer crossed his arms over his chest. "You alone out here?"

"My husband's gone for help. We were trying to get to the hospital when the car died, and—"

"You won't be birthing your baby on Chricton's roads." He nodded back to the truck.

A second Enforcer appeared from the passenger's side. He was smaller than the first. From the lines on his face, Sherri guessed he was also a good decade older. "Get this woman out of the road."

Breathing deeply, Sherri thanked him for his kindness.

"Move her to the sidewalk. Then get this car out of our way."

"You're not going to take me to the hospital?" She knew they wouldn't. This was just part of the act.

"Your child is not our problem."

The older Enforcer stepped forward and scooped Sherri into his arms. Finally, Axle could see what they were up against. He nodded across the street at Auver. Auver nodded back. Then Axle raised three fingers into the air. He lowered them one at a time.

Three.

Two.

One.

Axle swung around the side of the building with his gun at arm's length. It took him less than a second to get a bead on the younger Enforcer. "Hands on your head!"

Raivine followed suit.

"You, too!" shouted Auver, his gun aimed at the man holding Sherri. "Put the lady down and put your hands on your head."

Sherri flailed her arms and legs violently as the Enforcer jerked around, trying to assess the situation.

It would take a shot to the face to kill either Enforcer. The rubber from which their uniforms were made was actually a form of armor that would harden to become as impenetrable as eight inches of steel upon sudden impact.

However, despite this protection, the younger of the two dropped to his knees and cupped his hands behind his head. He was probably inexperienced and lacked confidence in the protection the uniform provided. Axle took the Enforcer's gun and kicked him to the ground.

Abot cowered behind a brick wall, afraid to come out.

Raivine and Auver had their guns aimed straight for

the remaining Enforcer's face.

"Put her down now!" Auver growled.

The Enforcer looked back at his partner, only to see Axle on top of him, tying his hands behind his back.

"Let me go!" Sherri screamed.

"Put her down!" Raivine insisted.

Before the Enforcer could decide what to do, Sherri whipped her hand around, punching him in the face. He stumbled backward. She fell to the road and rolled away. When she came to a stop, she yanked off the tape holding her gun to her thigh.

"Hands on your head!" Auver repeated.

Blood from the Enforcer's nose dribbled down his chin. With a snarl, he grabbed his gun from his belt and fired for Auver's heart.

Auver dived out of the way and the bullet ricocheted off the building behind him.

"Hey!" Raivine shouted. She was kneeling, had one eye closed, and was using the other to aim her gun. When the Enforcer turned, she fired.

The bullet struck his armored shoulder. The rubber shielding transformed instantly to its altered state. The bullet was deflected, drilling a hole into a nearby wall instead of the Enforcer, but the blow knocked him back a step. Then, a moment later, the uniform became soft again.

Sherri's shot, which followed, had the same effect.

Furious, the Enforcer aimed for Raivine.

That's when Abot finally made his move. Scared as he

222

was, he rounded the building in an awkward spin, yet kept his hands steady enough to hit his target. Because the Enforcer had heard Abot shuffle his feet, he had glanced over his shoulder just before the marksman pulled the trigger. The bullet ripped through the Enforcer's broken nose. He fell to the ground, dead before he hit the cement. His face was unrecognizable from all the blood.

The battle was over. One of the Enforcers was hogtied, cursing and screaming; the other was dead. But Abot kept his gun drawn until Auver walked over to him and slowly pushed it down. "It's finished."

Axle removed his knife from his boot and Sherri took it from him. "I'll do it." She walked over to the faceless Enforcer. Blood dripped slowly down the sides of the helmet onto the road. It pooled around the one blue eye that had not been destroyed by the gunshot. She could see the empty hatred in that one eye.

She closed the eyelid, then stripped off his uniform to the waist. They needed his chip because their simulators wouldn't get them past The Palace wall. Once she'd undressed him, she kneeled down and used Axle's blade to slice through the flesh of his forearm. She didn't have to start sawing until she reached the bone.

Axle turned to Raivine. "Get the car out of here."

She kissed his cheek. "I'll see you soon, Father." They both hoped it wasn't a lie. She darted to the vehicle. The engine roared as it came to life. Tail lights lit up. Tires squealed. Moments later, she was gone, speeding down the cracked, decaying roads of Drekar.

Axle watched her until she was out of sight, then he and Auver investigated the contents of the armored truck. With a crowbar they found hanging on the inside of one of the rear doors, they pried open crate after crate. Most contained cases of beef. A few had packages of dehydrated milk. In one near the back, they found an assortment of cheeses.

"After we've taken down Chricton, we're bringing this food back to The Resistance," Axle said, then glanced at his watch. The first countdown had been timed for this intersection. A new one would keep them on target for The Palace. The truck was expected there in—

"Six minutes, twenty-two seconds."

They were already behind.

"Top speed, we're still twelve minutes from The Palace gate," Auver said.

Axle hopped out of the truck. "Sherri!"

"What?" she asked, still sawing through the bone. Her hands were completely covered in blood.

"We've got to go."

"Almost there." With one quick motion, she jerked the arm against the elbow joint, breaking the remaining bone. Flesh tore and the blood from the forearm drained onto the street. She ripped off the bottom third of her dress, wiped her hands with the torn fabric, and tied it around the end of the severed limb so that the entire wound was covered.

After giving the hand to Axle, she tore off the tape that

held the pillow to her stomach, dropped the pillow on the ground, and climbed into the back of the truck.

Abot looked at the Enforcer who was still alive, drawn by the obscenities he was shouting, and then noticed that a teenager was watching them from half a block away. His leather jacket hung on only one shoulder.

"Hey, kid. It's okay, we're—"

Before Abot could finish, the teenager ran down an alley. While Abot couldn't be sure exactly where he was going, he was headed in the direction of The Palace gates. "Axle!"

"What?"

"We've been spotted."

Whether the teenager suspected they were part of The Resistance or feared they were common thieves, Abot had good reason to be concerned. Many of Artubal's citizens believed the lies Leon spouted and considered The Resistance to be composed of nothing but traitors and thugs.

This misconception had been solidified when a handful of men who had joined the movement just to have their chips removed went on a crime spree through the city two years earlier.

"Get under the truck," Axle said to Auver.

Auver put on a pair of thick, leather gloves and slid underneath the vehicle. He wrapped his boots into the frame, pulled himself up to the truck's grimy underside.

Axle climbed into the driver's seat, Abot into the

passenger's. "Hold this," Axle said, tossing the Enforcer's arm into Abot's lap.

Abot cringed with disgust as the severed arm dripped blood into the seat cushion.

CHAPTER 22

There was only one way through the gate. When it was closed, there seemed to be no entrance at all, as if the road just stopped when it met the polished, steel wall at the perimeter.

Having passed the teenager, Axle pulled up to the post. The truck was fourteen minutes short of its expected arrival. While that made Axle uneasy, it was not likely to cause alarm.

Axle took the hand from Abot and stuck it into the opening on the steel tube. A blue light flashed. The wall slid open.

Another mile of road stood between them and The Palace. Around the distant fires, Axle knew, huddled men and women who hoped to become servants for The Palace.

He drove the truck slowly forward until he was on the other side of the wall, where he was stopped by the raised hand of an Enforcer. "Contents check!"

His partner walked with short, military steps toward Axle's window.

While this was probably standard procedure, Noor

hadn't mentioned it. If he had, Axle and Abot would have changed into the Enforcers' uniforms after the last confrontation.

In reflection, that seemed like it should have been part of the plan from the start.

But there was no time for second-guessing. They'd come too far to back out. It was kill or be killed from here on.

The Enforcer suddenly halted. "Who are—"

Axle drew his gun and fired before the question could be finished. The Enforcer's face exploded as he fell back onto the sand.

Immediately, from the front of the vehicle, the dead man's partner fired back. The bullet hit the windshield, but didn't penetrate the glass.

Slipping partway out his window to return fire, Abot took the man out in one shot. Straight through the face, just like the others. Axle slammed down hard on the gas, looked in his rearview mirror. The dead guards quickly disappeared into the blackness behind them. To their right, they passed a child sleeping inside an overturned car; she had a dirty red blanket pulled to her chin and was shivering from the cold. The car was nothing but dented rust and flattened tires.

"Nice shot," Axle said. "Good to see your courage up. You'll need that."

Abot kept the gun in his hand, ready, but didn't say anything.

They passed a small tent on the left, where a hairy, old man roasted some sort of meat over a fire.

The tires on the truck were worn; they slipped, struggling for traction. The shocks were nearly exhausted.

Axle and Abot bounced in their seats. Sherri pressed her hand against one wall to brace herself. The vibration challenged Auver's grip on the undercarriage; he tightened his fists to keep from falling.

This was as far as their plan had taken them. The rest of the way, they were going to have to wing it. Thank God for Noor's map.

~

Abot watched the man by the fire in his rearview mirror. He had joined The Resistance because he hated seeing people suffer. And these people were suffering. Terrified of being sentenced to the Artubal Cells off the coast if they turned to crime and unqualified for military services, many citizens with nothing to barter and no job prospects came here to the desert to await their chance to serve inside The Palace. It was a hard life. Fewer than half of those who showed up here ever made it inside.

Those who still supported The Palace said it was their own fault that they had to live this way. They were uneducated or incompetent. Sure, things were bad. But if you had a skill, if you were good at something, you could have a job.

Like the rest of The Resistance, Abot didn't believe that it was this simple.

He stripped off his jacket and rolled down the window. Cold wind rushed in. He shivered. But he knew the servants-in-waiting needed the jacket more than he did, so when they passed another fire, he tossed it out the window.

There must have been three dozen men and women gathered there, all filthy, all sitting with their hands close to the flames.

As the coat drifted slowly down through the desert wind, they ran to investigate. Several of them grabbed it at the same time, tugging possessively on it. They shouted at each other. They barked obscenities. An extra coat was a valuable thing in the desert. But the stitches tore, the sleeves ripped off, and they were left with only a shredded, useless garment. They dropped the coat and scrambled back to the fire, where they stared hatefully at each other.

~

The team was closing in fast on The Palace. Once they got there, they'd have to get inside, spread out, disappear into stairwells, make their way up sixteen floors to Chricton's chambers, and kill him.

"We can do it," Axle said, without taking his eyes off the road.

Abot responded with an unenthusiastic "Yeah."

They were only a quarter of a mile from The Palace.

Lights at its base illuminated the giant, glass walls—walls that grew wider as they climbed toward the sky.

Overhead, the moon cast its glow freakishly across the sand.

Axle began to make out bubbles of black glass protruding from The Palace walls. Had there been no drugs swimming in Brian's bloodstream earlier, he would have seen them, too. He would also have been able to discern the fifteen-foot robotic spiders that patrolled the stretch of desert between them and The Palace.

Like the guards at the gate, these were another surprise. They moved fluidly on long black legs, and were often masked by shadows.

"Abot?"

"Yeah?"

"Keep your courage up."

Abot hesitated. "I will."

"Once we get inside, you've got to come out shooting just like you did back there at The Palace wall."

"I know."

"We're all going to die if you don't."

"I know."

Axle watched the building grow large in front of them, as he kept an eye on the spiders. He was looking for any sign of trouble, because he knew that only hair-trigger reactions would keep them alive.

Reluctantly, he slowed his speed. They were close now. Very close . . .

He could imagine being inside Chricton's chambers, the look of horror on Chricton's face when he pulled the trigger.

This is for you, Raivine.

Suddenly, two metal doors at the end of the road slid open to welcome them. The bright light from the loading bay spilled onto the road. He was now confident that they wouldn't have any problems getting into The Palace; they were still being mistaken for wanted guests.

Then brighter lights flashed on from inside the loading bay. Ten or fifteen of them, maybe more. Small, circular fog lights.

At the same time, the spiders shifted in unison to face the armored truck.

Axle eased off the gas. "I'm sure everything's fine, Abot," he said, talking more to himself.

He recognized the fog lights as headlights, and the headlights as motorcycles. Behind the motorcycles were the shadows of men—Enforcers. Engines roared. The Enforcers pulled out of the loading bay. They weaved around each other on their elongated bikes, on and off of the road.

The spiders simultaneously moved forward—one step, another.

Axle swore as he slammed the gas pedal to the floor.

They picked up speed.

He shifted from third to fourth to fifth gear. Ninety miles-per-hour over the bumpy, cracked road.

"We're not going to make it through all of them," Abot said.

Axle didn't say anything.

"We've got to turn around."

This time Axle responded. "The boy." The one who'd seen them steal the truck. Though the men at the gate were dead, he had somehow warned The Palace.

Axle pushed the truck as fast as it would go. Past more fires and tents and overturned cars. Straight into the belly of the beast. Head on with the motorcycles. Head on with the charging spiders.

Underneath the truck, Auver was able to angle his head so that he could see the lights on the motorcycles reflecting off the road.

"Axle, we've got to turn around!" Abot said again.

Their only chance—

"Did you hear me?"

"Start shooting, Abot!"

"Axle, we're not going to make it! We got to turn around!"

The two hundred feet between them and the Enforcers was closing rapidly.

"Where we can we go?" A day . . . two tops . . . and everyone in The Resistance would be dead if they retreated.

Suddenly, the front of the truck was sprayed with bullets. The left headlight cracked and went dark, then the right one.

Axle swerved, attempting to get out of the line of fire. The tires slipped. The truck bounced violently. The faster he went, the harder the vehicle was to control.

In the brief silence that followed, Abot summoned all his courage, leaned out the window a little more carefully than he had when the truck had been still, and fired at one of the Enforcers.

Right on target.

Just like always.

The Enforcer's neck snapped back as he was thrown from the bike. Unmanned, the bike wobbled until it fell, tumbling end over end and finally sliding to a stop, throwing up plumes of sand.

But Abot was unable to fire off another shot before they were assaulted by a barrage of bullets. They were coming from machine guns that had been designed for and welded to the bikes.

The bullets put new cracks in the windshield, but still didn't break it. A short series ripped off the driver's side mirror.

Axle swerved again.

One of the robotic spiders, moving relentlessly toward them, stopped. Its oval body tilted and rotated. From where pinchers would have been had it been a living creature came a bright blue laser.

Axle jerked the car to the right and the laser singed the road.

The technology used to fire a laser was cumbersome

and extremely heavy. No one man, nor even two, could manage such weight. The spiders could, though.

~

Underneath the truck, the sudden turns proved to be formidable adversaries for Auver. His fingers again slipped from the two steel pipes he was holding. Just an inch. Then another. Although his feet were securely locked in place between those same pipes and the underside of the truck, the muscles in his arms began to burn.

A spider came up from the other side and fired another laser. Axel jerked the truck again. Auver's right hand slid completely off the pipe, but he recovered quickly.

~

Axle drove straight through the group of motorcycles. They veered off the road—some left, some right—to avoid a collision. Their tires spun in the sand as they turned around to come up from behind.

One hundred feet from the open bay door. Seconds stood between them and The Palace.

A spider fired another laser.

Axle jerked the truck to the left but stayed on course.

~

Underneath, though, Auver could no longer hold on. Both hands slipped from the pipes. His desperate scream became one of terror and pain as his head slammed into the road. Hair and flesh were skinned from his scalp. His ankles broke as his feet slid out. His body twisted sideways and a rear tire rolled over his thighs.

~

The truck bounced violently when it rolled over the body. Abot looked in his rearview mirror, which was still attached, and saw Auver lying on the cement.

If not dead, he was all but.

Then an Enforcer stopped long enough to pull his handgun from the holster on his waist and fire a round into Auver's chest.

All Abot could manage to say was, "Auver's down." His words were filled with such grief that he needn't say more.

~

The news rattled Axle, but he refused to show it. Instead, he focused his pain on Chricton. He tried to imagine how much sweeter their victory would be in the wake of his friend's death.

Almost inside the bay, Axle slammed on the breaks. Not quite soon enough, though. The truck slid through the bay doors, collided into the wall facing them. Had they been several feet to the right, they would have gone soaring through the large, gaping doorway that led to the parking garage.

Though this was the same bay through which Brian had come earlier, the men in brown uniforms were nowhere to be seen.

The hood buckled, the truck shook. Axle pounded his fist on the rear wall of the cab to tell Sherri they were inside.

She swung open the back door and stepped out, gun pulled. With the Enforcers rapidly approaching on their motorcycles, she darted to the stairwell and up to the walkway. Axle and Abot followed close behind.

To Axle's surprise, the Enforcers refused to fire their machine guns into the bay. If they had, they could have ripped the three intruders to shreds.

Axle and Abot went through one doorway. Sherri went through another. At the first hallway, Axle and Abot split up.

Each had the same task, so their odds of success would be greater if they separated. It would only take one bullet to kill Leon Chricton.

CHAPTER 23

The halls—gleaming white, bright enough to hurt his eyes—were deserted. Everyone was asleep.

Originally, Axle was looking for a storage room or a stairwell. Somewhere he could duck out of sight until the Enforcers had cleared the floor and moved on. None of the doors were marked, though. Just plain white doors with silver door handles. Doors that could lead anywhere.

He took several sharp turns in hopes of losing the Enforcers. One white hallway led to another. More unmarked doors.

To no one would he admit that he was afraid. To no one would he say that he was ashamed of how he had treated Brian. He had to be strong. He was the rock on which The Resistance anchored their hopes.

He made another turn and was suddenly face to face with three Enforcers. He fired off a shot, missed, and ran back the way he had come as they returned fire.

Another turn. Another white hallway.

They were close behind him, but not within sight.

Then he saw the elevator Noor had drawn on his map.

The gleaming silver doors were polished daily. A pair of buttons beside it told him he could go up or down.

Knowing this was his best chance for escape, he pushed the top button, took aim at the corner which he had last rounded. If anybody came, he would start firing.

Sweat dampened his shaggy, gray hair and dripped down his forehead. Heavy stains had formed on the cotton shirt underneath his armpits. His gray, furry jacket seemed to soak up his energy and hamper his movements, but he dared not take it off; to leave it would be like leaving a trail for the Enforcers.

He heard footsteps echoing nearby.

The elevator doors opened. He slipped in without being seen.

Perhaps by only seconds.

Then, he hit the button for the seventeenth floor. It no longer made sense to find a place to hide when reaching Chricton would be so easy.

The interior of the elevator had mirrored walls, a glass ceiling, and a white tile floor. Because he hated his haggard reflection, he quickly turned his attention upward. Through the glass top, he could see the steel runner to which the elevator was attached—there were no cables at work here. The small lights that lined the glass ceiling only illuminated several feet of the shaft; beyond that, he could see only blackness.

If he had wanted to hide, his only hope would be to squeeze through the polished iron grate in the floor.

It was two feet by two feet—a tight fit for Axle, though not impossible.

Through it, he saw the steel arms that held wide steel slats in place four feet below the base of the elevator. They were for the workers who moved in and out of the grate when something needed to be repaired or the runner greased.

The floors passed quickly. At thirteen the elevator stopped with a thud. Something had gone wrong. Desperately, he pried at the grate. It was attached securely in place by four screws, and Axle had nothing he could use to open it with.

The doors parted.

Adrenaline racing, Axle drew his gun on two Enforcers and stepped through the doorway shooting. He killed them both before they could return fire. Behind him, the outer doors closed on his right heel. While his foot acted as a wedge for those doors, the ones that were a part of the elevator closed all the way.

With a hum, the elevator began to descend.

Not wanting to lose the elevator or be stuck on another floor with Enforcers, he holstered his gun, and spun around as far as he could while keeping his heel between the doors. Summoning all his strength, he pushed the doors apart. Then, without gauging distance, he jumped.

He fell two floors before he hit the glass top. The glass was thick and well-made; it didn't break. However, the blow knocked the wind out of him.

Ten.

Nine.

He was an easy target where he was. His only chance of hiding was to get under the elevator. He slid off the glass top, carefully lowering himself between the passing floors and the side of the elevator.

Seven.

Six.

Holding onto the greasy rim where the glass met the steel frame, his fingers slipped. He fell faster than the elevator descended. He saw the steel slats. They were his last chance of surviving. Without thinking, he grabbed them.

His whole body jolted when he stopped falling.

His grip was far from secure. He scrambled desperately to get a better hold and to pull himself up. The odds were better than good that on the bottom floor the steel slats would all but slam into the elevator's grinding motors. If he wasn't on top of the slats by then, he would be crushed or ripped in half—or both.

~

Unlike Axle, Sherri found a stairwell with relative ease and began sprinting the floors. At seven floors up, she heard a door open above her.

She froze.

Another opened below.

She was surrounded.

The sound of footfalls echoed around her like thunder.

She began to panic. She grabbed the door handle for the seventh floor. Before she could pull it open, she heard a loud mechanical thump. Every door to the stairwell had locked simultaneously.

Now her only option would be to fight her way out. After quickly weighing her options, she darted down the stairs. She could run faster down stairs than up them, putting the most distance between her and the two teams of Enforcers, giving her the best chance of getting out alive.

Three Enforcers met her one flight below. She got off a shot fast enough to kill one, then a bullet hit her in the leg and she tumbled the last two steps to a landing.

Another shot pierced her heart.

~

Fifth floor.

Fourth floor.

Third floor.

Axle pushed himself up until his torso was lying on one of the slats. His legs still dangled.

Second floor.

He got one leg up.

First floor.

He got the second leg up.

The elevator stopped.

The grinding machinery that Axle feared was inches away. However, the limited light in the shaft that bled through the grate above only made a little bit of it visible.

He heard the elevator doors open and quietly shuffled his body along the slats to a corner.

Above him, an Enforcer stepped in, looked around, then stomped on and tugged at the gate to make sure it was secure.

"Clear," he said, as he stepped out.

Axle breathed a sigh of relief.

He removed his penlight from a coat pocket to examine the machinery that had almost killed him.

The greasy gears ranged from three to six feet in diameter and were each a foot wide. Steel cases housed electronics. Metal tubes running along the walls held electrical cables.

~

Unlike Axle, Abot tried his luck with one of the unmarked rooms. He hoped to find somewhere safe, perhaps a storage room, where he could wait out the initial uproar.

No such luck. However, he knew it wasn't storage because of the large glass window that comprised the wall opposite the door. Without it, the room would have been pitch black. The pale moonlight that seeped in from outside made visible a closet, a door that no doubt led to a bathroom, some sparse furniture, and a bed.

While almost all the details of the room were hidden, the bed was parallel to the window, making the woman on it easy to spot.

Even though the figure was draped in shadows, her curves identified her sex immediately.

She opened her eyes. "Please don't shoot," she said without lifting her head from the pillow. "I'm no threat to you."

"Who are you?"

"I'm a servant. Nobody."

She sounded sincere. He lowered his gun. He couldn't kill a servant.

Once the weapon had fallen to his side, she asked, "Who are you?"

In a whisper, he answered: "I'm part of The Resistance. I'm here to help."

She sat up and turned on a bedside lamp. Her red hair was cut close to her scalp. A thin scar marred one cheek. She kept her bed sheet wrapped around her torso and squinted her deep purple eyes.

In the flood of light, Abot could see the sparse furniture was made of dark wood. Like in the hallway, the walls were white, but the floor was carpeted. Framed photographs of her with her family sat on the dresser. A large landscape painting hung on the east wall.

The furnishings were nicer than he would have

expected to find in a servant's room.

"I haven't heard any alarms," she said.

Abot didn't know how to respond to that, so instead he asked, "Do you mind if I stay here a while, until things cool down?"

She nodded, and patted a hand on the bed. "Come sit down."

He glanced around the room one more time, still trying to decide if she might be a threat. But if she was a threat, she'd have a gun under her pillow . . . or in the dresser . . . she would have already tried to shoot him.

Of course she would have failed—he was too quick—but she would have tried.

He sat down. "How long have you been here?" he asked.

"A long time."

"You must have been taken from the desert when you were very young." He held the gun in his lap.

She looked at it. "That makes me nervous. I don't like guns very much."

"Don't worry. It won't go off accidentally."

But she was unable to take her eyes off it.

"How old were you when they brought you in?"

Footsteps thumped loudly outside her room. She glanced worriedly at the door. Once they were gone, she said, "My mother wanted to work here. I was probably five or six."

"Thanks for letting me stay here."

"Stay as long as you need to. You're fighting the good fight, right?"

That almost sounded like sarcasm to Abot, but it couldn't be. "Right."

She looked at the gun again. "Good. I'm glad to hear that." She smiled.

A minute or more passed in silence. No footsteps outside.

With every second, Abot felt more confident about the room he'd selected and more comfortable with the woman in it.

They looked at each other, then both looked away.

"Please put the gun down. I see so many of those around here."

Radiant purple eyes.

She was so innocent.

"Sure. Since it's bothering you that much." He laid the gun on the opposite side of the bed from her, still within easy reach in case someone else charged through the door.

Then he wondered, "Why wasn't your door locked?"

There was a flip-lock above the door handle on the inside. She could have used it if she wanted to.

"Chricton doesn't like us to lock our doors. Some of the servants that have . . ."

"What?"

"Get beaten."

She reached over him, across, slowly so as not to

startle him. She put one hand on the gun. The sheet fell slightly to reveal just a little cleavage and he could smell her skin. "I'm just gonna put this on the nightstand," she said.

Perhaps because he trusted her, or perhaps because he was distracted, he didn't stop her.

She picked up the gun and moved back into her seat. Just before putting it on the nightstand, she asked, "How many of you are there?"

"You mean inside The Palace? Just a few of us."

"*That's* why there wasn't an alarm."

"What do you mean?"

"Well, if you'd come with a whole army, they'd have woken all the Enforcers."

She was still holding the gun, Abot realized. She had told him she was going to put it on the nightstand. "Maybe I should take that back," he said nervously. "I'd feel safer."

"I bet you came to kill Leon Chricton."

"Give me the gun back."

He was just about to jump on her, rip the weapon from her hand, when she spun it around, placed her finger on the trigger, and fired two shots into his chest.

Mouth slightly parted, eyes suspended in a state of shock, he rocked forward and collapsed to the floor.

Then, with the sheet wrapped around her, she walked to the callbox by the door, pressed a button, and announced his death. She also needed somebody to come clean up the mess, she said.

~

Stuck beneath the elevator, Axle hoped that his comrades were doing better than he was. He knew he should assume the worst, though.

When the elevator doors opened again, a woman stepped on. Through the hole in the grate, he could see she was wearing black pants tucked into black boots and a gray, long-sleeve shirt. Her red hair was cut short and she had a scar on her right cheek.

She pressed a button and the elevator went up. He counted the floors. They stopped on seventeen. Chricton's floor. She got out.

Directly below Axle were the exterior doors for sixteen. If Leon Chricton was in his chambers—and the arrival of the woman suggested he was—Axle was only one floor from the man he came to kill.

Getting to him, however, would still be challenging.

Stuck underneath the elevator, he had no idea how he would get out of the shaft. He couldn't jump to the narrow ledge in front of the doors that led to the fifteenth floor without expecting to slip and fall to his death. Even if he could successfully make the jump, he wouldn't have the leverage he'd need to wedge the doors open.

Then a solution came to him . . . and it was only a little less risky than jumping.

He took off his jacket and dropped it down the empty shaft so that it wouldn't obstruct his movements.

As agile now as he was at thirty, he locked his legs around the center slat, ankle holding ankle. Quickly, he rotated himself around the slat so that he was hanging upside down by his feet and hands. He released his hands and hung upside down.

With his back to the doors, he lifted his head up so that he could see them. He reached out and grabbed hold of the seal where the doors met.

Once again calling on all his strength to fight back the doors, he wedged them far enough apart to get his fingers between them.

He grunted as sweat dripped off of his forehead, falling into the emptiness below.

If the elevator moved right now, he would certainly die.

Slowly, he pushed the doors open enough to get a foot in, maybe a little wider. But that was as far as he could manage while hanging upside down.

Putting all of his strength into his arms, holding onto the doors as tightly as he could, he unknotted his ankles from around the slat.

His body flipped one hundred and eighty degrees in less than a second. His feet slammed into the shaft. Pain soared through his toes, and he scrambled until he got a foothold on the ledge. Breathing hard, worried that at any second the elevator would be summoned to a lower floor and crush him, worried that there were Enforcers lurking on the fifteenth floor outside the elevator, he wedged his right foot between the doors. Then, squeezing his torso inside, he used his hands to push one door and his back the other.

Suddenly, his left foot slipped on the ledge and he fell face-forward into the hallway. Rolling onto his back, he pulled his gun from his pocket.

The hallway was empty.

He got to his feet, took three deep breaths to slow his heartbeat, and summoned the elevator down to him.

Seconds later, he was inside, on his way up to seventeen. He kept his gun up, ready to start shooting as soon as the doors opened.

When they did, though, there was nobody to fire at. All he saw was a lobby, eight-feet square, and another door opposite the elevator. Unlike the elevator doors, this one was made of black oak and had a small stained-glass window at eye level. All four walls were painted a creamy brown. The ceiling was black, with dozens of tiny lights, twinkling like stars, hanging from thin wires.

Just before turning the door handle, Axle worried the door might be locked. If it was, a rattle or squeak from the handle might alarm Leon Chricton.

~

On the other side of the door, the decor had remained

unchanged since Leon had inherited command of the territory from his father, Roi Chricton, at the age of twenty-four. Roi had died from a prolonged cardiac condition, during which he'd suffered a series of small heart attacks. With his father in good spirits just before the final attack, Leon had been emotionally unprepared for the loss. Confronted with suddenly being the youngest ruler of the territory, he had felt compelled to take bold actions that would quickly elevate the territory to new heights of success and make his father proud.

It was this drive that had given birth to the Honesty Chip. What better way could there have been to drive the territory up that hill of success than by cutting crime?

Although the plan had not been popular when he first announced it, he rode out the unrest quietly—letting people complain, letting them protest—until his vision had been realized. *Sometimes the best choices for the people are not the popular choices*, his father had told him, and he repeated it to himself several times while he waited for his citizens to see the advantages of the chip.

In fact, the idea had been conceived in the very room he stood now.

Windows, curved like bubbles, lined every exterior wall of this inspirational chamber. Burgundy curtains covered every window. The room had two leather couches on one side and a third on the other. A glass-top table, knee high, was positioned between them. Soft string music pumped through speakers overhead. Colorful, ancient rugs from the western territories were strategically placed on the hardwood floors to complement the furnishings. The room was lit by a series of soft bulbs in the ceiling.

Chricton's living space totaled fifty-three-thousand square feet in all and the other rooms were equally stunning.

Daria Strost, the redhead Axle saw through the grate in the elevator floor, had been his lover before she'd led the attack on The Fountain a month back. To Leon, the attack was tantamount to betrayal, perhaps even worse since she'd led the attack on the very same night he'd asked her not to.

The only reason he hadn't had her executed was that he loved her.

He knew she was emotional and unstable. Although he'd shared everything with her until that moment, he should have kept to himself his reasons for deeming the club off-limits. She hadn't needed to know that he'd agreed no harm would come to Brian at his hand in exchange for The Mystic's help in winning the war. She hadn't needed to know that the Fountain was where Brian would first appear in this world or that it was a venue Raivine frequented; he'd understood The Mystic had revealed her association with the club by accidently only. Although he'd been guarded about sharing his knowledge of The Resistance, The Mystic had assumed The Palace's intelligence team was already aware that Raivine often went to the club.

Fortunately, although the attack had strained Leon's relationship with The Mystic, the agreement had remained intact since Brian had survived.

The agreement was important to Leon because only a few days before he'd made it, he'd learned that his demand for Moriba's surrender had been rebuffed. Although he thought they must be weary of the war, their territory growing weak as his was, their exact words to Leon's representative were: "Never. If Artubal does not fall at the hands of Moriba, they will fall from the inside."

Leon had already learned from Noor that Moriba was slowly arming The Resistance. They were secretly funneling the weapons into the city by first shipping them across the ocean, then having sympathizers import them as goods marked for other purposes. However, before Moriba's response, he hadn't believed they would have considered The Resistance a significant ally. From what Noor had told him, their numbers were too small.

Perhaps Moriba believed the underground movement bigger than it was. Certainly they didn't yet know Leon had sent men to the bus terminal to steal the weapons they'd been sending.

Whatever the reason for their faith in The Resistance, Leon was confident it was misplaced and he had not wanted to waste his dwindling resources fighting a small band of rebels underground. He'd wanted only to get the weapons so he could send them to his men on the frontline. Therefore, he'd had a small team quietly remove the debris that blocked access to the basement and had instructed Noor to gas the guards upon his order. Even if he had changed his mind, though, his promise to The Mystic had been made before his men had reached the stockpile, ensuring that Brian and the rebels were safe.

When Daria arrived in his chambers, he was mulling over whether he had made the right decision by prioritizing the war over The Resistance. The fact that they felt confident enough to plan such a brazen strike on The Palace suggested that maybe he hadn't.

Dressed in his signature black shirt and pants, Leon had been sipping wine from a goblet before Daria came in. He offered her a glass, which she bluntly declined. Then she told him that she'd killed one of the intruders and he told her that the Enforcers on duty had killed another.

"There's one left," she said. They knew this from an Enforcer's observations at the bay.

"This is an outrage," he said. "Noor should have warned us they were coming!"

"Maybe he's changed his mind about what side he's on."

Leon considered the possibility. Someone who'd betrayed his own people could not be relied upon for loyalty. "Maybe he has."

"I think we need to take them down now. All of them. Before things get worse."

Leon drank the last of the wine and put the goblet down on the table. He used one hand to brush his long black hair away from his face. He stepped through a door on the west wall and returned carrying his gun. It was polished to a shine, always loaded. In case any of the intruders actually made it all the way upstairs, he wanted to be ready for them.

To Daria, he said: "Do it. To hell with The Mystic. I want them all dead. Chase them into their rabbit holes. Kill them. Get the sympathizers, too." He sighed and smiled at her in a way he hadn't since before the incident at The Fountain. He stepped closer. Putting one hand on her cheek, he gently kissed her lips. "This time you have my blessing."

Just then, three bullets ripped through the wood around the doorknob. Axle kicked and kicked again, breaking the knob off completely. The door flung open. He charged in with his gun pulled, spotted Daria, spotted Leon.

Immediately he ascertained that she was unarmed and thus focused all his attention on his target. He fired once. The bullet slammed into Leon's chest and threw the ruler onto his back.

Leon screamed. In shock, he couldn't yet feel the relentless alarms being sent by his nerve endings or the warm blood draining across his chest. He fired back. Three shots. The first two lodged themselves into the wall by the door. The third shot tore through Axle's shoulder.

~

Axle stumbled back but didn't fall. He was buoyed by the joy of success. He'd come here for Raivine, for Sherri, for Abot, for Brian . . . for all of those underground, for all of those who needed help. And he had accomplished his mission. . . .

Then, Chricton fired another shot into his gut. He doubled over and collapsed to the ground.

~

Leon fired one more shot before the gun slipped from his weakening grip. This one skipped across the floor, marring it, and pierced the nearest leather couch. Knowing the intruder was no longer a threat, Daria ran to Leon. She dropped to her knees, cradled his head in her lap. "My God!" she screamed. "Don't die. I'll get our best doctors up here. You'll survive this, I promise."

But the blood was draining from his chest too quickly. He gargled out a few unintelligible words and then stopped breathing.

Daria's heart ached. "Nooo! Noooo!" She wrapped her arms around Leon's corpse and rocked back and forth.

Behind her, Axle had rolled onto his chest and was attempting to crawl back to the elevator.

Before Axle made it out of the room, however, Daria picked up Leon's gun, crossed over to him, and fired the remaining bullets into his back.

Boom! Boom! Boom!

She pulled the trigger another six times, even though the gun was out of ammo.

With the gunshots ringing in her ears and blood seeping onto the rug from Axle's and Leon's wounds, Daria fought back her tears and searched Axle's body for weapons. She found the knife in his boot, pocketed it, and vowed to avenge his death.

CHAPTER 24

Brian pushed himself up the brick wall, fled the alley, and hurried to Flanders' house. People stared at the lab coat; they stared at his bare feet. They pointed at him from the safety of their cars; pedestrians moved out of his way. A mother pulled her daughter close to her chest, backed to the edge of the sidewalk; her big red lips pursed in disgust.

He ignored all of it.

He ignored the aches that came with every step. He ignored his throbbing hand. He ignored the cold wind that whipped his face and soared up the coat.

Two miles he walked.

When he reached his neighborhood, he darted through back yards, hiding in the shadows. He didn't want neighbors to see him arrive. He didn't want anyone to question the Brian-of-two-days-ago why he'd been outside in only a lab coat. By the time he got to the Flanders house, he was winded. He was also exhilarated. He knew what he had to do.

As he had expected, the two-story Victorian was quiet. No police tape. No cops. The burglary hadn't happened yet. The only signs of life came from the porch light that John Flanders turned on every night at dusk and the moths that were attracted to it.

Without a key, Brian knew he couldn't go through the front door. He couldn't possibly explain to the Brian-of-two-days-ago what was happening, nor did he want to try. He worried that any contact he had with himself might alter the future, possibly keeping him from ever meeting Raivine.

What would happen to the last two days then, he didn't know. He suspected he would simply forget all about the other world. The chip would disappear. The scars would heal up. And he'd be back in the PR department, scribbling out a new press release.

So far unseen since he entered the neighborhood, he hurried around to the back of the house.

Reluctant to waste any time searching for a rock that would be big enough to do what he wanted, he took off the lab coat and wrapped it twice around his fist.

He checked the pocket dangling close to the ground for the bottle of pills. They were still there.

He sucked in his breath, held it, and fired his fist through one of the six small windows on the rear door. The glass shattered and fell to the floor.

He reached a hand through the broken window frame, managing not to incur further cuts, and unlocked the deadbolt from the inside. Afterward, he shook the glass out of the lab coat, put it back on, and quietly stepped over the threshold.

Inside, the house was still, quiet. He listened for sounds of life for almost a full minute before moving again.

Once he was sure he hadn't awoken anyone, he climbed the stairs, avoiding those that creaked, and walked down the shadowy hall to his bedroom.

The handle squeaked softly when he turned it. Fortunately, the hinges on the door rotated silently.

In the bed, barely illuminated by the light from the window, the Brian-of-two-days-ago slept. He knew it was a deep sleep, because it had been his sleep.

As he looked at him, he was momentarily struck with a sense of nostalgia and a longing for the innocence that used to be his.

Quickly, he shook off those emotions. They wouldn't help him save Raivine.

He stealthily moved to the closet where he found a pair of jeans, a tee shirt, and a dark blue sweater. When he finished dressing, he put on the worn tennis shoes he kept on the top shelf.

What mattered was that the Brian-of-two-days-ago not notice the clothes were missing, so he grabbed things he didn't like, things he only wore on laundry day.

Leaving the lab coat lying on the bedroom floor, he closed the closet door and tiptoed to the edge of the bed.

The Brian-of-two-days-ago rolled over, mumbling something.

Brian's body locked up. He thought he'd been spotted. Then he was amused to find out that he talked in his sleep.

He knelt down, removed his wallet from the jeans on the floor, and took a twenty. He'd notice that later, but wouldn't wonder too long about it.

Halfway done, he told himself.

~

From the other side of the upstairs hall, John Flanders opened his bedroom door. He'd heard a noise.

~

Brian dug through the front pockets of the jeans on the floor until he found an old receipt. He removed a pen from a drawer on the nightstand and wrote on the back of it: *The police will get here in time.*

The letters were more jagged than was his normal handwriting because his right hand still throbbed from the surgery.

Stuck with an odd sense of déjà-vu (if it could, in fact, be called that), and suddenly needing to prove to himself that he could change Raivine's destiny, he added the word "Promise" at the end.

It was a little change, not one that would affect his past actions when he found the note, but it provided him with the confidence he needed. The past . . . future . . . whatever you wanted to call it . . . could be altered.

Watching the Brian-of-two-days-ago for any signs of consciousness, terrified of what might happen if he woke up, Brian slipped the note under the bed and grabbed the .38 Chief's Special.

He remembered how angry he'd been with the burglar. If the gun had been available, he *would* have shot him.

Then . . . who knows? Maybe he'd have been arrested. Maybe, despite shooting the burglar, he still wouldn't have saved John. And if he allowed the Brian-of-two-days-ago to shoot him, then both the old man *and* Raivine might suffer the tragedies circumstance had first plotted for them.

He had to take it.

He had to take it and get out of the house as fast as he could.

While he regretted that he could not save them both, he feared that trying to do so could be as damaging to his past as leaving the gun.

And it wasn't just Raivine who would be affected if any change to his past prevented him from traveling to the other world. There were so many people, so many children, he could save with the pills he had.

It was a tough decision, but it was the right one. As much as it pained him to let John die, Brian tried to comfort himself with the knowledge that John had lived a full life.

God forgive me, he thought, as he pushed the guilt from his consciousness.

He picked up the lab coat, put it on over the sweater. Then he checked one last time for the pills and shoved the gun into his jeans and under his sweater. When he left the room, closing the door behind him, the Brian-of-two-days-ago was still sound asleep.

~

On his way back down the stairs, he saw light seeping out of the hallway. It was coming from the kitchen, he realized.

Flanders was downstairs!

Either he'd heard Brian break the glass or the murderer was close, or . . . or both. Maybe the only reason Flanders was downstairs at the time of the robbery was because he had heard Brian break the window, he thought.

While he knew John's death wasn't entirely his fault, he now felt responsible in a way he hadn't before. And the guilt of perhaps causing John's death was somehow worse than the guilt of not trying to undo it.

Suddenly, his previous logic seemed hollow, flawed. Maybe, just maybe, he could save both Flanders and Raivine. If he could, he'd find another way to make sure the Brian-of-two-days-ago took the first pill, starting the journey he was now on.

With the murder certainly only moments away and the guilt of responsibility upon him, he had to try.

He descended the last of the stairs quickly. Once on

the ground floor, he could see Flanders and the burglar in the kitchen, facing off. The burglar had come through the same door Brian had, and the door was wide open. His pan-flat face and beady brown eyes were unreadable.

Both men were frozen. Neither had expected to encounter the other. But the stalemate wouldn't last long. Brian had already seen the aftermath.

Why the burglar would choose a house that already showed signs of a break-in was beyond him. Maybe the burglar was hopped up on something, not thinking clearly. Maybe he thought the window had been smashed in a game of catch. Or maybe he just didn't give a shit why it was broken.

The burglar's reason for choosing John's house was irrelevant, though. All that mattered was that Flanders was alive . . . at least for the moment.

Acting on instinct, he ducked into the den, still unseen. He heard movement from the kitchen. "Why'd you have to come downstairs, you old fuck! I could have been in and out without any trouble."

There was a loud thump and dishes rattled.

Softly, Flanders begged the burglar not to hurt him.

Brian knew he would have to act now if he hoped to save his friend. He grabbed the heavy, wrought-iron candlestick off the nearby table. He hoped to knock the intruder out and leave with everyone still alive.

As he did, he wondered if this was how the candlestick got moved the first time. But before he could dwell on it, he was in the kitchen.

The burglar had Flanders pressed to the counter, with his hands wrapped tightly around the old man's neck. He mumbled repeatedly: "Nobody can see my face. Nobody can see my face. Nobody can see my face. . . ."

Flanders pawed at the burglar's wrists, but he was too weak to break free. He gasped for breath. His eyes bulged.

As quietly as he could, without slowing down, Brian slammed the candlestick into the intruder's back like he was swinging a bat.

In his plaid shirt and khaki pants, the burglar arched backward. He let go of John's throat, but he didn't scream. Instead, he spun around and yanked the candlestick out of Brian's hand just as he was going for a second blow.

With his attention completely off John, the burglar swung for Brian's head.

Brian ducked and retreated several steps, trying to figure out how to gain an advantage.

The burglar closed in. He swung the candlestick upward as he attacked, ready to bring it down hard on whatever he hit. But when he swung high, he cracked the shell on the overhead light, casting the room into darkness. Only the dim glow from the street lamps outside provided any remaining visibility.

Brian picked up a chair and threw it at the burglar. One leg hit the burglar in the stomach, knocking the wind out of him, before it clattered to the floor. He stumbled back a step.

The Brian-of-two-days-ago would be awake by now. Brian was running out of time if he wanted to get out of the house without confronting his former self.

In a desperate, last ditch effort, he ran straight for the burglar. He planned to grab him, knock him to the ground, rip the candlestick from his hand.

Before he could get a hold of him, though, the burglar grabbed his sweater and, using Brian's own momentum, threw him out of the way.

Brian hit the countertop. His face slammed into the wooden cabinets above it. The gun jabbed his groin. His knees buckled, and he fell to the floor.

Before Brian could get up, John fled into the hallway, toward the front door. Forgoing his fight with Brian, the burglar chased the old man down and whacked him hard across the skull.

John fell in such a way that wedged him between the walls of the narrow hallway. The intruder whacked him again. And again. Three more times.

Back on his feet, Brian could hardly believe that he'd failed. He'd had no time to rush the burglar before the final blows had been delivered.

He'd failed!

Twice he'd failed.

Flanders was dead, he had no doubt. His feeble body couldn't take that much abuse. Especially not right to the skull.

Trembling, angry, full of vengeance, Brian pulled the

gun from his pants. He locked on his target just as the burglar turned around.

Faced with the gun, the burglar froze.

Brian focused all of his pain, exhaustion, and hunger on the man in plaid. He was sick with himself for failing Flanders twice. Without a thought given to the consequences, he pulled the trigger.

~

Although the gun was loaded, had been loaded ever since he'd first put it under the bed, it didn't fire. And when it didn't, the burglar's courage returned. He mumbling something under his breath and attacked, candlestick up. But Brian unexpectedly stepped into his attack, kneeing him in the crotch. The burglar groaned and fell.

However, Brian knew he wouldn't be on the floor for long. And the Brian-of-two-days-ago would be coming downstairs soon. Losing the old man twice had multiplied his determination to help Raivine, so he couldn't stay to serve the justice the burglar deserved.

With the gun tucked into his pants, his legs weak, he ran. He didn't want to be anywhere near the house when the cops showed up.

For five blocks, he darted down dark neighborhood streets. They dumped him out onto the busy Trilite Road. When traffic cleared, he crossed, heading to a small grocery store on the other side.

He shed the lab coat outside the store and tossed it onto a bench. The woman inside working the register had puffy cheeks, dotted with acne. He asked her where he could find latex gloves and she directed him to the back of aisle three. He also needed a piece of paper, an envelope, a pen, and a stamp. All he could get here were the gloves and a pen.

With a latex glove shoved in his front pocket, he hurried back to the road where he waved his arms wildly at every cab that passed.

Nearby bars brought a lot of business to the cab companies, so there were always a few taxis floating around the area.

When one finally stopped, he climbed in and told the driver to take him to the Embassy Suites. Even if he'd had a full night's rest and a big meal, he wouldn't have been able to walk there in time.

The driver navigated the streets with all the speed of a turtle, despite the light Sunday night traffic. Twice, Brian asked him to speed up. "Sure," the driver said. "You the boss." However, he increased his speed not one mile-per-hour.

Frustrated, Brian stopped asking. He reminded himself that no matter how slow the driver went, it was faster than walking, and would likely be faster than hunting down another cab.

He settled into the rear passenger seat and watched the

buildings crawl past. An air freshener dangling from the rearview mirror attempted to mask the lingering stench of someone's vomit.

Then Brian worried about what would happen when he reached the other dimension.

Three days ago, he would never have imagined himself surviving everything he'd been through. He had been a quiet kid in school, never been in any real fights. The loss of his parents to a fire had been a tragedy, but the only one he'd ever suffered before John was killed. So he felt he had good reason to worry. After all, he was just a guy who worked in a PR department. No matter how strange things had become, he wasn't anyone special. And he didn't know much longer he would last before his body finally gave out on him.

When he arrived at the hotel, he walked through the lobby, past the front desk, to the bathroom. He locked himself in one of the stalls and used his teeth to gnaw off one of the fingers from the latex glove. When he was done, he threw the ruined glove on top of the toilet tank.

Inspired by the movie he'd seen several days before, he poured as many pills into the latex finger as he thought he could swallow. Not even the entire bottle would be enough to bring back everyone in The Resistance. But if his plan worked, he'd at least save Raivine, Axle, and some of the children.

After removing one more pill for his trip over, he recapped the bottle and knotted the end of the latex finger.

That pill he stuck in his left front pocket. The bottle and the latex finger he put in his right.

With all preparations made, and trying not to think about John's murder, he exited the restroom and walked up to the front desk.

"Can I help you?" asked the man behind it. He was wearing a navy blue suit and a striking red tie, both of which looked immaculate.

"Yeah. I, uh, I have a friend who's gonna be checking in soon. I have something I need to leave for him."

Suddenly, the man was at a computer terminal punching keys. "Certainly, sir, what's his name?"

"Oh, he hasn't made a reservation."

"You're sure he's coming to this hotel?"

"Positive."

"Sir, if he doesn't—"

"He told me he would be here," Brian said, and got a shrug for a response. "Can I leave something for him?"

"Very well. Since you're sure."

Then Brian talked the clerk out of two brown envelopes and some hotel stationary. The first note he wrote was short, to the point. Since, with his last note, he'd proven to himself he could change the future if he wanted to, he felt no need to prove it again.

The note said: *Take one as soon as you can. Trust me. A friend.*

He slipped the note and the pills into the first envelope and handed it back. "His name is Brian Dore."

After the clerk said he would take care of it, Brian went to work on the second note. In it, he wanted to tell the whole story, but had neither the time nor the paper for something so long. Besides, the shorter it was, the more believable it would be.

He addressed the note to the attention of Peter Stark, a reporter for the *Atlanta Journal*. The two had spoken often since Brian had started work at Omega. If anybody would listen to him, Stark would.

It read as follows:

CEO OF OMEGA HIDING DOUBLE LIFE

In the last three days, I have been kidnapped and tortured for reasons that are still unclear to me. I know only that Mr. Maine is behind it. You know me well enough to know I'm not paranoid and that I would not waste your time. While I have escaped, I am still scared for my life. Please investigate. I might not be the only victim. He keeps a lab on a secret floor below the building. I only call it a lab, because I don't know what else it could be, unless it's a torture chamber. If I can, I will call soon with more details, but don't wait around for that. Thank you.

When he finished, he sealed it in the second envelope and addressed it to the newspaper.

Then, with little more effort, he bought a stamp off the

clerk and convinced the sharp-dressed man to include the letter in the hotel's outgoing mail.

Brian concluded his conversation with a "Thank you" and returned to the bathroom on the opposite side of the lobby.

Like before, it was deserted. He had only his reflection in the mirror to watch him.

He removed the latex finger from his pocket and placed it on the sink. His only other pill he fished out of his left pocket and swallowed.

His hands started to shake. He had a couple of minutes before the drug would take effect. Worried he might choke trying to get it down, he dared not swallow the latex finger too soon.

Just because he'd seen someone do it in that cheap cop flick didn't mean *he* could do it.

He turned on a faucet and splashed his face with water. *You can do this. You can do this.*

I will *save Raivine's life.*

When his stomach started to feel queasy, he knew the shift would happen soon. He picked up the drug-filled finger, leaned his head back, and closed his eyes.

He got the tip of it into his throat without a problem. He massaged the muscles in his neck with one hand to inch it down.

His stomach grew angry. He started to tremble. The transition was almost upon him.

You can do this.

He worked the muscles in his throat faster. He suppressed the urge to vomit. He needed to breathe.

He got the latex finger all the way into his throat. He filled his hands with water from the sink and poured it into his mouth to ease the latex finger along.

He needed to breathe!

Then the shaking became spasms. Suddenly, he couldn't swallow. The latex finger was in his throat but he didn't know if it was deep enough to shift with him. He'd wanted to get it all the way into his stomach. That wasn't going to happen.

But worse—

He needed to breathe!

He fell onto the bathroom floor, hit the tile hard.

CHAPTER 25

Brian couldn't wheeze, couldn't cough. The bathroom dematerialized into blackness, and the ruins of the club in which he had first appeared faded in, out, and back in again.

When everything stabilized, when he could feel the cement beneath his feet and see the dark sky through the jagged hole in the wall, he rolled onto his hands and knees.

Stomach acid surged into his throat.

He hacked, tongue out, like a cat with a hairball.

Dreamy shadows pushed at the corners of his vision. He was going to lose consciousness soon if he couldn't cough up the latex finger he had swallowed.

Finally, in one last desperate effort, he reached his right hand into his mouth. The surgical scar stung as it scrapped against his teeth. With two fingers, he fished for the tail of the latex finger, continuing to hack, found it, and dragged it up his throat.

Once it was out of his mouth, he let go. It fell onto the dusty floor. His right hand dropped back to the ground to help support his weight.

Stomach acid coursed over his tongue and dribbled out of his mouth.

He stayed as he was, thankful to be alive, breathing deeply until he had enough oxygen to stand.

He was thrilled that his plan had worked, and scooped up the latex finger.

At first, he didn't recognize where he was. Wherever he was, it was cold. Very cold. He started to shiver.

As his eyes adjusted, he saw beyond the rubble immediately before him to the bar. He recalled Raivine hovering over him, then helping him escape. He remembered the explosion that tore a hole through the wall, the terror and confusion that followed as people fled. At the time he had no idea what had drawn those men. Now, as he thought back on the events that had occurred at Raivine's childhood home, he suspected that it was his fault they had come. He had no chip back then.

Behind him, somebody lit a match. The bright sizzle of light illuminated the room. He turned around.

Working with his left hand, the robed one slid the match through a hole in the base of a lantern on the ground. The flame caught the wick. He closed the hole to keep the breeze from extinguishing the light.

Then, also with his left hand, he picked up a pile of rags by his feet and threw them to Brian. Reacting on impulse, Brian caught them.

He worried that the robed one's presence might lead to more torture.

"I told you not to come back," the robed one said in his deep, mysterious voice. "I told you Chricton's problems weren't yours to worry about."

Brian couldn't say anything. Nor could he take his eyes off the robed one long enough to see what he was holding.

"Put those on," the robed one said. "You'll need them to keep warm."

In a daze, yet compelled to follow the robed one's instructions, Brian unrolled the rags to find gray, cotton pants and a gray, burlap shirt. "Thanks," he said, tentatively.

He wasted no time putting them on. While he dressed, the robed one also tossed him a pair of leather shoes.

"I couldn't get a jacket," the robed one said, after Brian had his pants on and was slipping the shirt over his head. "But you won't freeze to death now."

The long sleeves on the burlap shirt compensated for its lack of comfort with warmth.

After Brian had put on his shoes, a perfect fit, and laced them up, the robed one sighed and said, "You're doing an admirable thing, but you're not going to be able to save her."

Horrified that the robed one had once again been able to get inside his mind, and equally horrified that he had known exactly where to find him after his third jump, Brian could only say, "Excuse me?"

"All you're going to do is make things worse for

yourself."

Still uneasy, though boosted by the courage he'd recently tapped into, Brian asked, "How do you know so much?"

Underneath his hood, where the lantern barely lit his mouth, the robed one smirked. Then he dissolved into nothing.

Brian jerked his head right, left, afraid that something bad was about to happen.

"I know everything."

The voice was behind him. He spun around to see the stranger.

"Since you've chosen to disregard my warning and return, there are things I must tell you. . . . There was a man from your world here before you. Not years or even days ago. Only . . . before. I learned of his suffering.

"He was not the man he had thought himself to be. He had grown up in an orphanage and been homeless through his early teenage years."

For reasons Brian couldn't explain, he could see himself as this boy. Sleeping on streets and in parks. Eating from the garbage bins of fast food restaurants.

"Like many others, he had been abducted and taken to an underground laboratory. Nobody would miss him because he was homeless. So, for his captors, he was the perfect guinea pig. They put him through unspeakable experiments, locked him in a depravation tank, tortured him when he refused to cooperate, and subjected him to—

"This is Omega you're talking about," Brian said, remembering the lab he had been in, although he couldn't understand where the other bits came in.

"Yes. And when they were done, he believed he was somebody else. A different person with a different past and a different name. He was given a home where they could monitor him.

"Brian, that person was you."

Flanders' house.

"The chain of events you're living through now were put in motion long before you, as you know yourself, were involved."

"But, how?"

"I'll get to that," the robed one said, and continued with his story. "After school, you were given an internship at Omega so that you could be watched more closely. The goal of the experiment was to discover how effectively somebody could be reprogrammed."

Your father would have been proud, Flanders had said, when Brian was given the internship. *It's only too bad about the fire.*

"For years, they watched for cracks in your psyche. When the burglar killed John, those cracks began to form. He had chased you to your room. The you who had lived through these events before grabbed the gun from underneath your bed, aimed it at the bedroom door, and pulled the trigger. But it didn't fire. So you climbed out the bedroom window and jumped to the ground, where the cops found you.

"For days afterward, you wondered why it didn't fire. You told yourself that it hadn't been used in years. Of course the gun didn't work. Bu something didn't feel right.

"Then, memories of your parents began haunting your dreams. They twisted, morphed—perhaps 'fractured' would be the best word—into disjointed scenes from the times you were homeless and tortured. They seemed so real you had to talk to somebody about them.

"Since you were living with Shawn after John's death, you talked to him. And he filled your head with all kinds of conspiracy theories about how Omega might be involved. Of course, you mocked him, told him to be serious. However, it made you curious.

"Then, late at night, still at your office desk, hours after everyone else had gone home, you managed to crack into encrypted company files with tricks that had taken months to learn.

"At first you refused to believe what you found. But as you dug further into the files, the cracks grew deeper, and clues became evidence."

Brian wondered whether the story he was hearing now could be true. With everything he'd lived through the last few days, he couldn't say with certainty it wasn't.

"When you found the documents that detailed the experiments you had undergone, you learned John was a company employee hired to watch you. You also learned the gun had been provided by the company and tampered with so that it would never actually fire. It was intended only as a tool to remind you of the company's control over you. Hours of hypnosis had ensured its effectiveness . . . until you were crouched in your room, holding it, aiming for the door, trying to kill the man who had just killed John. When it didn't fire, it was no longer threatening. It lost its power.

"After you finished your research, you had to see the underground lab for yourself. You had to put to rest any doubts. So you made a point of bumping into Steven Lester one day on his way out of the elevator. Abruptly, hard, and fast . . . apologizing profusely. You grabbed his arms, his jacket. He couldn't possibly keep up with where your hands were. In the midst of the activity, you reached into the pocket of his lab coat and removed the key that would take you to the subbasement.

"There you found the white hallway from your dreams, a keypad you knew the code to from your research, and, on the other side of the door opposite the elevator, the horrific electric chair and other oddities.

"Unfortunately for you, your actions were discovered and you were dragged back into the lab. This time, instead of using you for mind control experiments, they tested drugs on you. All sorts of drugs. Sometimes the side effects left rashes on your skin; once you bled from beneath your eyelids. Finally, they tested something on you called Diaxium. Twice they sent you here before the relationship between time and space slipped backward and you woke up on the night of Flanders' murder, in an empty lab, much like I suspect you did the last time you returned to your world."

Perhaps for dramatic effect only, the robed one vanished and reappeared on Brian's right. "In that timeline, you returned to save Raivine, just like I suspect you did now."

From Brian's left, he said, "You failed."

Then he asked: "Do you remember the night they took you? The first time? You'd been leaning against a wall behind a fast food restaurant."

"No, I . . ." He stopped short as he saw himself in the parking lot.

"It doesn't matter. . . . He left the lab as you probably did, in a white lab coat, carrying a bottle of Diaxium. He left the note and the pills at the hotel, as you must have."

A sudden strong breeze whipped at The Mystic's robe and tousled Brian's hair. "Don't make his mistakes."

Brian tried to get his mind around the robed one's story. It answered a lot of his questions; on some levels, it even made sense. It explained the impossibility of the notes he had found before he had left them. But that didn't make it true. The Mystic had proven already he could get inside Brian's head.

"I know you don't believe me yet. You will."

No longer worried the robed one would harm him— whatever his intentions, he didn't seem interested in violence—Brian decided to challenge the story. "Where is the other me now?"

"He lives in your future."

"But you live in my present, so how could you have met him?"

The robed one shifted, ending up behind Brian.

"If I can transcend space, do you not think I can transcend time?"

"So you came back through time specifically to stop me from making his mistakes? Why?"

"He hoped that, since you were his past, you would go home and not return. And if you did, he hoped he would be set free from this world. Your actions would become his past, and he would be released from all the horrors here you have yet to experience.

"Since you didn't, I want you to remember something: I came back through time at your request. It's not too late to make the right decision." The Mystic held out one hand. "Now give me the pills."

Brian's left hand tightened around the latex finger. "No. I can't. I need them. If I've really sent you to me, you know that I need them."

"They'll only get you in trouble."

"I can save Raivine."

"You won't."

"I can save the children."

"You'll fail."

"I can't give you the pills."

282

Then some unseen force tugged at Brian's fingers until they opened. He tried to close his right hand over his left, but found his arm wouldn't move. He was paralyzed. The latex finger flew from his hand to the robed one, who caught it and ripped it open. He removed one pill before dumping the others onto the ground. Brian tried to stop him—he tried a front-on attack, but his feet wouldn't move either. All he could do was scream as the robed one ground the pills into dust.

Afterward, he walked forward and dropped the remaining pill into Brian's frozen hand. "I know you will still go into the city," he said. "But this is your only way home. You will not shift back like you did before because you now know this world is real. Each time you traveled here, your subconscious accepted more and more of it. That is why your second trip was so much longer than your first. Now that you've fully come to terms with this world, you don't have the ability to shift dimensions without the drug. Not even I could do that."

Brian was taking short, ragged breaths, no longer able to scream. The robed one had locked up Brian's vocal chords so he would hear every word.

"I'm not doing this to hurt you, I'm doing this to help you. With only one pill, I hope you will be more cautious than you were last time. Think hard before you give it away."

The robed one dissolved as he had before, but did not reappear.

CHAPTER 26

As soon as the robed one was gone, Brian Dore's fingers snapped shut on the only pill he had left, as if they were still struggling to hold onto the latex finger. His vocal chords opened and he screamed, startling himself into silence. Then he spun turned twice, certain the robed one was still nearby.

He wasn't.

The pants the robed one had given him had one pocket on the left side. After checking to make sure he hadn't accidentally crushed his remaining pill, he slipped it into the pocket.

While he was still suspicious of the robed one's story, he believed that the mysterious stranger wanted him to live.

He circled behind the bar, where he found a pile of rubble blocking the entrance to the tunnel. So, instead, he exited through the hole that had been torn into the wall when the club was attacked. After getting his bearings, he turned right, and started walking. Wind blew scraps of paper and trash past him. An empty brown bag shuffled down the road until a metallic green car crushed it under a tire. Streetlamps flickered. A drunken couple, the girl holding onto the guy's torso, staggered past.

He made all the right turns and ended up in the wrong alley. The streets looked too much alike. There was no grate where he expected to find it and he had to start over.

Then, in the distance, he heard one of the bug-like choppers flying over the city.

With increasing urgency, he found another strip that he thought might be the one he and Raivine had walked. Unfortunately, it, too, took him to the wrong alley.

He tried twice more, but still got no closer to his destination.

Above the buildings, he strained to see The Palace. The bright spotlights in the sand trickled along its glass. If he didn't hurry, somebody in there was going to hurt Raivine.

He found his way to another familiar street and tried again. This time, he recognized with certainty the sign over a small shop—all squiggly letters, like those Raven had pointed to in the photo album—and the flyer stuck to a lamppost next to the door.

Although he couldn't read either one, they were enough to give him his bearings. He turned so that his back was to the lamppost and started into a jog. He dodged the few pedestrians he encountered.

Somewhere along the way, the cloudy sky opened up. As rain fell, the chilly night air sought refuge under his skin.

Once at the right alley, he found the grate. Shivering, he slammed his heel against the top of it, hoping to break whatever mechanism held it in place. The clang that followed echoed up the buildings surrounding him. He slammed his heel into it again, and did so repeatedly until the vibrations rattled his leg to the knee.

There had to be an easier way to open it.

He got on his hands and knees and felt along the inside of the grate. On one end he found the mechanism that would open it when coming up from below. Beside the mechanism, perhaps a part of it, he felt a tiny switch. With trembling fingers, he worked it forward and backward, but nothing happened. Then he pushed it to the right.

The grate groaned and opened. Kneeling on the street, he looked down the alley to make sure no one was watching before he went down the hole into the ventilation shaft.

Once again, the grate closed on its own.

Rain dripped in from above. Beyond the few feet of tunnel made visible by the streetlights, he could see nothing.

He had only his memory to trust.

Using his right hand to guide him, firmly placing his palm against the wall with every step, he moved out of the light.

Not even his frosty breath was visible here.

Fear of the unknown and fear for Raivine kept him

going, forcing him to walk faster than he otherwise would have. When his hand fell upon only air, he counted the first fork in the shaft. He needed the next one.

He could change the past, he told himself. He'd proven it. Despite what the robed one said, he would save Raivine.

He turned right at the next fork and followed it to the jagged exit which led into the earth. By now, the cold had seeped deep into his flesh, seizing his organs. His teeth rattled.

He stepped through the hole The Resistance had made, into a rocky tunnel. Still blind, he proceeded cautiously along the uneven ground. Using his left hand, he felt the rocks protruding from dirt walls. Tiny roots brushed his palm. The pressure of his touch compacted loose dirt or sent it tumbling to the floor.

When his hand fell upon the next opening, he climbed carefully back into the ventilation shaft. It was a straight shot from here to the library, as he remembered. But because the tunnel curved around, he could see no light bleeding in from above.

Several more steps, though, and he could. He walked faster toward the light, not daring to run for fear of tripping and breaking an ankle.

When he reached the hole beneath the library, he hoisted himself up. Everyone was awake, huddled in private conversations. The littlest children hung close to their mothers. In one corner, a baby cried.

Before he was halfway through the hole, however, they all stopped speaking and turned to look. Their eyes were filled with something he hadn't seen before from this band of rebels, something like . . . wonder . . . or fear.

With only the crackling fire to challenge his voice, he shouted Raivine's name. He crossed the room and opened the door to her chambers.

Inside, all of the candles were lit. She sat cross-legged on a pillow. Her eyes were closed. Her lips moved, forming mumbled words.

She was praying, Brian realized.

He hated to interrupt. The urgency with which she mumbled suggested something of great importance.

He closed the door, sat down in front of her. Her eyes never opened—she was too lost in her own mind to realize he was in the room. He gently put his right hand on hers and said her name softly.

Startled, she opened her eyes immediately. "Brian." Then she leaned forward and hugged him with all her might. When she let go, she slid her hands down his arms. Their fingers locked. "You is home."

"I need you to do something for me," he said, "before it's too late."

She looked at him, puzzled, and he realized that explaining the situation to her was going to be difficult.

She rubbed a thumb along the back of his right hand as if to comfort him. Slowly, her thumb stopped moving. She turned his hand over and saw the stitches.

~

She needed to get him to Dr. Shirgarmo immediately.
The chip was broadcasting his location. Wherever he went,
the Enforcers could find him. This made him a danger to
himself and everyone he was around. It had to be removed.
Especially in light of the recent attack on The Palace.

She dragged him to his feet. "Come!"

"But I have to—"

"Come!" she insisted again.

~

Dr. Shirgarmo was, as always, willing to help. He led
Brian upstairs, wearing only his lab coat and a pair of wool
pants. "Hmm, yes, hmm. Another chip."

The two bodies he'd previously worked on had been
removed from the lab. The organs he had wanted to keep
had been bagged, labeled, and stored in the giant freezer.

Nothing, however, had been cleaned. Surgical
equipment was everywhere. Long sharp knives were slick
with blood.

"It okay," Raivine said to Brian. "He take . . ." Then
she pointed to his hand, tenderly touched the scar on back.

She wanted to know how he'd escaped from The
Palace, but couldn't find the words to ask. Nor was it the
time.

Brian looked nervous, but he nodded. She sensed he understood what needed to be done. Without direction, he lay back on the table and closed his eyes. He didn't want to watch the procedure.

The doctor left the room. When he came back, he was wheeling a metal cart on top of which sat a sophisticated prosthetic hand and an axe. The prosthetic hand, which looked more machine than human, had been designed by the doctor and a sympathizer who was an expert in robotics. It was of average human size and had a steel tube that extended from its wrist. Inside the tube were rubber grips that could expand to secure the hand to almost any forearm.

The axe was clean because it was the only piece of surgical equipment the doctor had never needed.

Since the first chip he'd removed for The Resistance, he hadn't made another mistake. Even when he was drunk enough to see double, he'd been able to get the chips out without incident.

He attributed his consistent success, in part, to the haunting memory of that first death. It had been horrific, tragic. Every time he picked up his knife to remove an Honesty Chip, the memory of that death replayed itself. He could see the man foaming at the mouth, the violent tremors and spasms.

Although he was not certain at the time exactly what had happened, he'd since confirmed that the chip had released a miniscule amount of toxin into its host's bloodstream. And the only way to save someone after that had happened was to cut off his hand before the toxin worked its way up his body.

That's what the axe was for.

The cart, which had one wobbly wheel, he left within easy reach of where he would be working. He dragged over a stool and gathered his supplies: a small knife and two identical tools that looked like wire cutters.

With his supplies lined up on the metal table, he removed a rag from one cabinet over the sink, ran it under the faucet, and dabbed away the dried blood on the back of Brian's hand.

He observed the other wounds on Brian's body. "Quite a beating this boy's taken, hmmm?"

Without answering him, Raivine walked to the other side of the operating table and tightly gripped Brian's left hand. There would be no anesthesia available to him.

He squeezed her hand back and kept his eyes closed.

~

Brian's heart pounded ferociously, but he understood Raivine would not have brought him here if the surgery weren't critical.

He would give her the pill as soon as it was complete. Despite what the robed one had said, he had confidence he would eventually shift back on his own.

~

After attaching the telephoto lens to his glasses, Shirgarmo used the small knife to cut away the stitches. Brian clutched Raivine's hand tighter. Then, using his fingers, he grabbed the threads between his dirty nails and pulled them out.

"Hmmmm," the doctor said, for no apparent reason.

With his thumbs on the back of Brian's hand, he gently pulled the scar open. The wound had already started to heal. Brian screamed through clenched teeth. He leaned his head back. His legs shook, but he kept his right hand still.

The chip was now visible to the doctor. Its tiny clamps held it securely in place. Inside the needle on one end, the poison hibernated.

The doctor exchanged the knife for the wire cutters. With one in each hand, he wedged their lower blades between the chip's clamps and Brian's flesh. In every operation, this was a tight fit.

Brian didn't scream this time, but held Raivine's hand tight enough to slow the circulation to her fingers.

"It okay," she said, reassuringly. "It okay."

From here, the doctor simply had to cut and hold. When the wire cutters separated the chip from its clamps, he would lift the chip out before its internal alarm reacted and plunged the needle into the vein.

It was a relatively simple operation, as long as he

worked fast.

Then they heard choppers and loud voices outside. The noise distracted the doctor, alarmed him. He looked toward the door, as if someone might come barging through. Raivine looked in the same direction, filled with the same dread.

An explosion somewhere nearby vibrated through the floor. Unconsciously, all of Shirgarmo's muscles tightened.

Immediately, the computerized chip began to beep softly.

Brian opened his eyes, looked at Raivine. "What's going on out there?"

She didn't understand what he had said and didn't have time to figure it out. Looking at Brian's hand, the doctor and Raivine saw the damage. When all the doctor's muscles had tightened, the fingers in his right hand had closed together ever so slightly. The movement was not enough to cut through all three clamps holding the chip on that side, but it had been enough to cut through one.

And like his surgery on Dox, one had been enough to set off the chip's alarm.

The needle extended and punctured Brian's vein.

At the same moment, gunfire echoed through the adjoining room. The door to the waiting room was locked. Somebody was shooting his way in.

There was no time to discuss what had to be done, to apologize, or even to warn Brian. The doctor picked up the axe and brought the blade straight down on Brian's wrist.

Brian screamed louder than he ever had.

Raivine pinned his shoulders to the table and jumped on top of him to hold waist down, too.

"It okay. It okay."

Using his axe like a broom, the doctor swept the hand onto the floor. He dropped the weapon. Blood sputtered out of Brian's wrist and Brian continued to scream.

Shirgarmo threw off his glasses, grabbed the prosthetic hand, secured Brian's flailing right arm, and shoved his bleeding wrist into the open end at its base. With the rubber grip that surrounded Brian's forearm still loose, the doctor flipped open a small panel on the wrist of the prosthetic hand. He entered a code on a series of small buttons and closed the panel.

The rubber grip expanded until the hand was securely attached.

Brian was in so much pain that tears formed at the corners of his eyes.

Outside, the gunfire stopped and they heard the door to the waiting room fly open, rebounding off the wall.

Though she couldn't see it, Raivine knew what was happening to Brian: Five metal pins had extended out of the prosthetic hand into Brian's wrist. Their high-tech design enabled them to identify his nervous system and attach appropriately.

Then the whole wrist of the prosthetic hand heated up, cauterizing the wound.

Shirgarmo ran to the door that divided the operating room from the lobby. All it had was a lock on the handle. He turned it, buying them only seconds.

The Enforcers pounded on the door.

He shouted for Raivine to run.

She wanted the doctor to come with them, but knew it was too late to save him. Just like she'd known the men were Enforcers. Something had gone wrong with the attack on The Palace.

Axle was certainly dead.

She grabbed Brian's left hand and yanked him off the table. "Come! Come!"

He shouted a series of things she couldn't understand and resisted at first. His eyes were cloudy with betrayal.

Bullets ripped through Shirgarmo's door and then Shirgarmo. He fell on the floor in a bloody heap.

Brian ran.

Raivine led him back through the basement, back through the hole that divided the tunnels, and headed in the opposite direction from which they had come.

She feared for the children and the families underground. The Haven would have been overrun with Enforcers by now . . . or would be very soon. So would all the other rooms. There was nothing she could do about that. All she could do was get herself and Brian out of harm's way. Once the attack was over, she would find a way to fight back, to avenge her father's death, but for now survival was a top priority.

CHAPTER 27

Brian followed her down new tunnels. Her penlight was on. The mustard rocks around him took on a new eeriness when combined with the dizzy spells that followed the surgery. His right wrist throbbed with greater pain than he'd ever known. He worried he might pass out again.

Though he didn't understand why Raivine had let the twitching doctor cut off his hand, he understood that she must have had a good reason.

They ran from one tunnel to the next. He wanted to stop her so he could force the pill down her throat, but the pill would take several minutes to work. If he halted their progress now, she might suffer more than a shattered kneecap and a sliced throat.

He would have to do it soon, though.

They ducked into a ventilation shaft. Heavy footsteps echoed down the shaft from behind them. How far sound carried through those shafts was anybody's guess, but the sound seemed close enough for Raivine to shout, "Come," and charge ahead as fast as she dared.

They made it to a vent unseen. It opened at the touch of a button. For the first time, Brian realized that these mechanisms had not been installed by The Resistance, but by The Palace for access by maintenance crews. Raivine sent Brian up the ladder first. He made it safely onto the street. She followed. Nearly halfway out, gunfire whizzed past her legs.

Brian heard it and offered her his hands. "Grab hold!" For the briefest of moments, he had forgotten about the surgery. He cared only about getting her to the surface alive.

She grabbed his hands. The fingers of the robotic attachment closed at his will. He grunted, yanked her up, fell backward. She landed on top of him.

His right wrist throbbed with fresh pain as she rolled off and shouted again for him to follow, but he was up quickly and on her tail.

~

They ran through the alley, around one of the long, blue corpse-keepers, crushing bugs beneath their feet. Overhead, the choppers sounded like a tornado.

At the end of the alley, more gunfire came at them from behind, forcing them onto the wider road. The shops were closed. The lights were off. Deserted cars were parked along the curb.

To the left, more shots echoed those which came out

of the alley. With one hand, Raivine grabbed Brian's shirt and dragged him between two cars. She glanced around the vehicles to see four Enforcers jogging toward them.

Raivine still had a lead of forty or fifty yards.

She held up a finger and told Brian to wait. Once she was confident that he would, she crawled around the car behind them on the side closest to the curb. From here, the Enforcers couldn't see her. She couldn't see them, either. The car was so rusty it looked like it might fall apart any second.

She tried the rear door. It was locked. She then tried the front passenger door. Something clunked inside as if loose, but it didn't open, either.

There wasn't time to experiment with another car. If she couldn't get into this one, they would be captured or killed.

She jerked the handle repeatedly, desperately. Each time, the cluck behind the metal got a little louder. Then there was a thud as the lock broke and the door swung open.

Following the thud came the shriek of metal against metal. The hinges that held the door in place tore free. The bolts grinded through the rusty frame and the door fell onto the sidewalk with a crash loud enough to draw the attention of the Enforcers.

"Come!" she shouted to Brian, as she crawled into the passenger seat. "Come!"

In the barrage of gunfire that followed, Brian ran,

ducking low, around the side of the car and through the open door.

Seated in the driver's seat, Raivine reached under the steering column and, holding the penlight in her mouth so she could see, fished through the wires that hung underneath. Axle had taught her how to hotwire a car almost two years ago, but this would be the first time that knowledge had come in handy.

Gunfire riddled the vehicle behind them and their trunk. It blew out the rear window. Brian ducked, scooting down in the seat to avoid being hit.

Raivine jerked the ends of two wires free and touched them together. The engine sluggishly turned over.

To get more room to pull out, she reversed and slammed into the car behind her. The bumpers locked. She switched into drive, floored the gas pedal. The wheels rotated without gaining traction. The Enforcers closed in.

Then the bumper tore loose, and they were moving. She sideswiped the car in front of them as they pulled out.

Brian flinched and jerked away from the open doorway. He grabbed hold of the seat with his left hand.

As they wound through the streets, Brian wondered where they were going.

A chopper overhead caught them in its spotlight and followed. Raivine swore in her own tongue and made a couple of quick turns, leading them down more narrow streets with barred windows.

Brian laid the prosthetic hand in his lap, unsure what

to do with it or how it worked. Then he remembered using it to drag Raivine out of the ventilation shaft. The fingers had moved at his command.

He fired off instructions to his nervous system, telling his fingers to close. They did. He opened them one at a time. As much as his arm hurt, the prosthetic hand seemed to work almost as well as his original ever had.

~

When Raivine and Brian escaped in the car, one of the Enforcers used the radio strapped to the wrist of his uniform to call for help. The message was then forwarded to Daria Strost.

She was underground, leading a team of thirty Enforcers in the mass slaughter of The Resistance, when she got word of the fleeing couple.

She was furious, and in killing felt she brought justice to Leon's death.

Around her, members of The Resistance screamed, running for hidey-holes, ducking into tunnels, desperate to escape. The few carrying weapons, stowed in jackets or boots, fired back in a futile effort to claim victory from overwhelming odds. The bullets couldn't pierce the Enforcers armor, though.

Every scream of agony, every death, sent her heart racing.

But as much as she relished the moment, things below

the surface were under control and she had a new priority. She instructed those Enforcers nearest her to accompany her back to the surface. They stepped on the lifeless bodies of women and children and shot anyone they could on their way out.

They climbed into the cars and onto the motorcycles they had left at the surface. Daria requested the coordinates from the monitoring chopper.

~

There was only one safe place Raivine knew to go: Orig. If Shirgarmo had been killed, she had to assume that all sympathizers had or would suffer the same fate. There was nowhere above or below ground within the territory to hide.

Since avenging her father's murder meant surviving and surviving meant running, finding a place to recuperate—a place where she could mourn her loss and Brian could heal—they ran.

But getting to Orig would be almost as difficult as surviving in the city. They'd have to cross hundreds of miles of desert. They'd have to face the unspeakable creatures that inhabited it. And if the car died before they arrived, they'd have to find water and food where there was none to be found.

But she still had to try.

It was their only hope.

However, they couldn't shake the chopper, and it wasn't long before Brian saw a caravan of Enforcers behind them. In cars and on motorcycles they came. He screamed the news to Raivine and pointed. She looked, but remained silent.

~

If they got outside the city limits, the Enforcers would retreat. Raivine knew there were too many risks for them to bother pursuing two runaways into the desert.

She kept the gas down. They had a sizable lead, but the Enforcers continued to gain ground.

On the long, straight streets, the shops that lined both sides of the road were closed. Eventually, the buildings turned into abandoned neighborhoods, the neighborhoods thinned, and then there was nothing.

Two miles farther down, the road took them to the city's perimeter, marked by a large steel wall that in all ways visible was identical to the one that surrounded The Palace. What they couldn't see was that this one extended ten feet into the ground to ensure the creatures that slithered beneath the sand were unable to get into the city.

Another difference between the walls was that this gate was motion-activated. One was not required to have one's Honesty Chip scanned to exit the city.

~

They closed in on the wall quickly. Raivine didn't slow down. Brian worried they were going to crash, but just in time the wall slid into itself and a moment later they passed from the city into the desert that surrounded it. As they breezed through a four-way stop, where every option except the way back appeared to be consumed by blackness, Brian noticed the sand ripple along the edge of the road, as if something moved underneath it.

~

When the chopper turned back, Daria insisted her crew keep going. "Drive! They're not going to get away."

Through the earpiece in her helmet, she heard an Enforcer say, "The desert will finish them."

With one hand on her steering wheel, she put the radio up to her mouth. "We have to be sure."

~

The Enforcers kept pace, continued to gain ground. Raivine was shocked. She was certain they would have given up by now. She looked at the gas gauge, but couldn't tell how much fuel they had left. One of the bullets had shattered the round glass dial.

Although their best chance for survival was to stay on the road, they wouldn't outrun the Enforcers. Fleeing into the desert might deter further pursuit, she decided.

She made a hard left. The car bounced violently over the ripples in the sand. Voices rose from those ripples, screaming in ghastly pain.

However, the Enforcers were not deterred. They turned into the desert after her.

~

Brian knew he had to tell her now. She had to take the pill. She had to flip over to his world. It was her only chance of surviving. He didn't know if previous actions might have already saved her a slashed throat, but if they had, her new fate could be worse.

"Raivine, I need to tell you something!" He had to shout to be heard over the noise of the engine and the disturbing shrieks that followed the cold breeze.

She kept her eyes on the road.

He removed his only pill from his pocket. "You need to take this!"

She glanced at it.

Suddenly, sand swelled into a wave in front of them. As the rolled over it, the car bucked, throwing the rear tires into the air. They came down hard. Raivine swerved to regain control, but didn't look back.

He thrust the pill toward her. "Take it! Take it now! It's your only way out of this!"

"We go!" she shouted back.

With the pill in front of her face, he said, "Take the damn pill! They're going to kill you if you don't!"

The car swerved and rocked.

"Do it!"

Then they went over another wave of sand and this time the passenger wheels were thrown into the air. As the car rolled onto the driver's side, Brian dropped the pill and pressed his hand against the dashboard to brace himself.

Raivine and Brian were tossed around. They hit their heads; their necks twisted. Finally, the car settled upside down on its roof.

Outside Brian's door, they saw what had flipped it.

~

The sand monster reeled back, throwing off the sand that had hidden it, and gave way to the most horrific sound Brian had ever heard. Wide jaw, sharp teeth. Below its hairy torso and clawed hands, it moved on a snake-like tail.

Over eight feet tall, it swiped a claw at the car. Brian crawled frantically to the driver's side while Raivine fought to open the door.

Another swipe from the claws, this one closer.

With a squeal, the door opened and they both rolled out. As soon as they were on their feet, they ran.

The sand monster roared, slithering around the car. So far it was the only one to appear. But because they travelled in packs, there would be others soon. If Raivine hadn't left her gun behind, she would have shot it.

To make matters worse, the Enforcers were still coming.

~

The creature was almost upon Raivine and Brian when Daria ordered it killed. She wanted to take down the two traitors herself.

~

The sand churned around Raivine and Brian. Two more creatures threw off their desert disguises thirty feet ahead. With sand-matted hair and glowing turquoise eyes, one was indistinguishable from the next. They slithered forward.

Raivine and Brian immediately stopped. She glanced from left to right, looking for another means of escape, but more sand monsters were coming up on the sides. Still underground, but coming.

Brian was certain he was looking into the face of death.

Then the sound of a machine gun split the night air with a rat-a-tat-tat loud enough to drown out the monsters' roars.

Raivine fell to the desert floor. Brian dropped to his

knees, covered his head, and glanced in the direction of the gunfire.

Eleven Enforcers, spread between three cars and six motorcycles, had taken up position in a semicircle fifty feet away. Machine guns were responsible for the spray of bullets.

The monster behind Brian wailed and fell face first onto the desert. The fur on its back was drenched with blood.

The two facing Brian and Raven dived for cover. One was shot through the chest before it could escape. The other ran with its brothers, not for destinations unknown as the Enforcers had expected, but straight for them.

~

Once they realized what was happening, the Enforcers tried to turn around and get back to the road. But it was too late. Six sand monsters rose up underneath the Enforcers' vehicles, toppling the cars and motorcycles.

In a fury, they smashed windshields and dragged Enforcers out of their vehicles, yanked them off their motorcycles and tossed them to the ground like ragdolls. Ripping limbs and snapping necks, they slaughtered the army. Only Daria had been lucky enough to escape.

As soon as she'd seen the sand monsters coming for them, she abandoned her vehicle and ran. Once at a safe distance, she couldn't help but turn to watch as her skilled, trained followers were ripped to shreds.

She was certain that once they were done with the Enforcers, the monsters would return to finish off Brian and Raivine.

They didn't.

Instead, they howled in unison, dived under the sand, and slithered away.

~

Brian and Raivine had been just as sure as Daria that the sand monsters would kill them. All three were surprised they were still alive as they watched the desert beasts leave.

It was a quiet, sobering moment that lasted some fifteen seconds.

Then, across a graveyard of overturned vehicles and shredded body parts, Raven and Daria glared hatefully at each other.

Almost directly between them stood the only car that had not been overturned during the attack. They both knew they'd find a gun inside it. No doubt there were others spread across the desert, but neither woman could be sure those guns wouldn't be clogged with sand, if they could even be found.

With the shock of still being alive over and the weight of survival upon them, both women broke into a sprint, headed for the car.

Raivine kicked up sand with ever step, willing herself to go faster. Faster than she'd ever run. Faster than she thought she could.

As she reached the open driver's side door, she slid on her knees, letting friction bring her to a stop. She was only seconds ahead of Daria, though.

She scanned the driver's seat and the floorboard, but was unable to find the gun before Daria slammed all her weight into Raivine, pushing her to the ground.

Sitting on Raivine's chest, Daria pinned her enemy's arms under her knees. Then she grabbed Raivine's throat with one hand as she took out Axle's knife from a small, leather pouch on the side of her belt.

Raivine recognized it from its distinctive human-shaped handle.

"You shouldn't have killed Leon!" Daria spat. "You're all going to die for that."

Just before she was able to drag the knife across Raivine's throat, a gunshot rang out from behind her. The bullet slammed into her back. Her armor kept it from penetrating her skin, but the force of the impact knocked her off balance.

Raivine seized the opportunity to throw Daria off of her and scamper away.

When Daria got to her feet, she saw Brian holding an Enforcer's gun. He gripped it tightly in his trembling left hand.

~

Elbows locked, arms out, Brian kept the gun aimed at Daria.

She and Raivine had been so focused on each other, neither had seen him run around to the other side of the car. Just when Daria tackled Raivine, he opened the passenger door and found the gun. He hadn't actually known what he was looking for until he saw it.

Before Daria could speak, he fired again. This one hit her in the stomach, knocking her back a step.

"Skin!" Raivine shouted. "Skin!"

Of course, Brian realized. Her face, the only exposed flesh.

Daria spun the knife in her hand, screamed, and charged, no doubt expecting to take the gun from Brian before he could kill her.

However, doing his best to aim, he pulled the trigger several times in rapid succession and managed to hit his mark.

Daria collapsed into the sand, dead.

After a deep breath, Brian let the gun fall to his side, then let it slip out of his fingers. It landed on the ground with a soft thud. But he couldn't take his eyes off Daria's lifeless body. As he stared at it, he realized that Raivine no longer needed the pill he'd brought for her—and lost. Daria must have been the person who cut Raivine's throat.

~

Raivine ran to Brian and hugged him. They were alive! More than that, her father had killed Leon! She knew she would miss Axle. She knew she would cry for him. But at least he had done what he set out to do so many years ago—he had given the territory a chance to start over.

~

Eventually, Raivine let go, stepped back. They realized they were no longer alone. The Mystic was standing five feet away, the desert wind ripping at his robes.

Trembling, Raivine grabbed Brian's hand.

"I'm not here to hurt you," he said to her in her language. "There's something I must tell Brian and then I will go."

Slowly, Raven nodded.

"Thank you," he said to her. Then, he turned his attention to Brian. "I told you about the Brian who was here before. I told you he sent me back in time to protect you. . . . It looks like I was wrong to have assumed you'd need my help. It seems you succeeded where he failed. Perhaps if you see what will become of you, you will do so again."

He raised his hands to his hood and both long sleeves

slid down his arms, revealing a robotic right hand. He pushed the hood back from his face; attached to the robe, it fell onto his back.

Brian could barely believe what he was looking at. It was *his* blond hair, *his* blue eyes. It was *his* face, only with more wrinkles.

Was it real? Was it a trick?

Then, as their eyes met, The Mystic said, "Don't become me," and crumbled to dust.

His prosthetic hand fell into the sand and his robe floated away. Seconds later, they vanished too.

This wasn't the sort of disappearance that suggested a shift from one world to another, or even a shift through time.

In a way that he couldn't yet explain, he understood that when his future self had revealed his identity, *his* future had changed. Exactly how it had changed, he didn't know. He only knew that he would never let himself become the robed one—and that he wasn't Brian Dore anymore, either. He was becoming something else, something new, something better.

CHAPTER 28

"You Mystic?" Raivine asked.

"No."

Raivine smiled. "Go," she said, and they did.

As they climbed into one of the Enforcer's cars, Brian looked back at the vehicle that had brought them there. He suspected with a little digging he could find the pill he'd meant for Raivine and take it himself to go home. He now knew with certainty he wouldn't be able to go back to his world without it. But he didn't want to. The life he'd had in his world wasn't his own. There was nothing to go back to. Here—he smiled back at Raivine—he had . . . something real.

~

Raivine started the engine and eased them carefully back to the road. Then she turned the wheel to face the city and slammed her foot down on the gas pedal.

No matter what she would find there, she no longer wanted to run. Leon was dead. It was time to rebuild

Drekar.

From the *Atlanta Journal*:

Justice for Human Guinea Pigs
By Peter Stark

Timothy Maine, CEO and founder of Omega Medical, Inc., has been found guilty of a long list of charges related to kidnapping, torture, and corporate fraud. He has been shackled with three consecutive life sentences to be served at the Forestware State Penitentiary.

"I hardly think that's long enough," commented John Fairchild, from the District Attorney's Office. "If I had it my way, he'd be in the gas chamber right now."

The verdict came after a surprisingly short six-hour deliberation on behalf of the jury and a trial that lasted just four weeks.

"The things Maine was doing to these people were practically a throw-back to the Dark Ages," Fairchild added. "They reminded me of the mind control experiments performed by the Nazis during World War

II."

The lead chemist at Omega, Steven Lester, who is wanted on related charges, managed to escape before being apprehended. He still has not been located. Nor has Brian Dore, who blew the case open eight months ago with a letter he wrote to this newspaper.

While no official comment has been made, nor charges filed, the police fear Dore's disappearance might suggest murder and are still actively attempting to ascertain his whereabouts.

PROBABILITY CHAIN:

THE CELL – PART 1

Available

October 1, 2014

Proof

Made in the USA
Charleston, SC
02 October 2013